NO MORE
US FOR YOU

ALSO BY DAVID HERNANDEZ

Suckerpunch

DAVID HERNANDEZ

NO MORE US FOR YOU

HARPER TEEN

An Imprint of HarperCollins*Publishers*

The Risk of Death chart on page 38 is based on figures from the National Safety Council, the U.S. National Center for Health Statistics, the Centers for Disease Control and Prevention, and the Office of Justice Programs. For further information, visit www.nsc.org; www.cdc.gov/nchs; www.cdc.gov; and www.ojp.usdoj.gov.

HarperTeen is an imprint of HarperCollins Publishers.

No More Us for You

Library of Congress Cataloging-in-Publication Data
Hernandez, David, date
    No more us for you / David Hernandez. — 1st ed.
        p.   cm.
    Summary: Isabel and Carlos, both seventeen, find themselves growing closer after an unexpected accident forces them to confront both the harshness and the beauty of life.
    ISBN 978-0-06-117333-2 (trade bdg.)
    [1. Friendship—Fiction.   2. Conduct of life—Fiction.
3. Death—Fiction.   4. Grief—Fiction.   5. High schools—Fiction.   6.   Schools—Fiction.   7.   California—Fiction.]
I. Title.
PZ7.H43174No   2009   2008019203
[Fic]—dc22   CIP
                                                            AC

Typography by Andrea Vandergrift
09 10 11 12 13 CG/RRDB 10 9 8 7 6 5 4 3 2

First Edition

FOR LISA

CARLOS

So there I was, sitting on my folding chair, my first day as a guard at the Long Beach Contemporary Museum, when a man walked in and stood with his back turned to me, arms dangling at his sides. At first I didn't know what he was doing, why he was looking down. I thought there was something on the floor that held his attention—a plaque I hadn't noticed, an air vent, some strange insect crawling silently across the hardwood. He spread his feet apart and lifted his head toward the ceiling, at the industrial pipes snaking up there, the light fixture angled at a large pile of bright green sand in the corner of the museum. He moaned. Then the urine came.

"Hey!" I shouted. I stood up from my chair and walked toward the man, half confused, half afraid. Maybe he had a knife. "What are you doing?" I said, which was stupid. I mean, it was pretty obvious.

The man ignored me. Urine splashed on the floor, his puddle growing bigger before him.

"You can't do that," I said.

The man looked over his shoulder and continued relieving himself. He was in his early thirties, with a goatee and a long, slender nose. His eyes were self-assured, sleepy, as if he'd been urinating in public all his life and was now bored with the act.

"Who says I can't?" the man said.

"I say."

"And who are you?"

"I'm the museum guard."

It was the last Sunday in January, and up until that moment I had been thinking what an easy gig this was, how little foot traffic there was, that people were probably at home reading the paper, mowing their lawns, or at church listening to a sermon.

And then this jackass walked into the museum.

"Nice jacket," the man said.

I had thought my suit and tie made me look professional, older and confident, someone who was doing things right. But after his remark I felt foolish, like I was playing dress-up.

The man wiggled his hips. The stink of his piss was pungent, slamming into my nose like the breath of a Dumpster.

"You're going to have to clean that up," I told him.

"Says who?"

"Says *me*."

"I'm sorry," the man said, "who are you again?"

"The museum guard!"

"Oh, right, right," the man said, zipping up. He tucked his shirt in and flicked the name tag that was pinned to my jacket. He patted my shoulder. "Good work," he said.

Ms. Otto, my boss, came running from the east wing of the museum, her heels clicking fast across the floor. She had a platinum blond bob and her bangs were snipped perfectly above her brows, ruler-straight. She was a small woman, petite, but her voice added weight to her presence. "What's all this yelling about?" she demanded.

The man turned around, surveying the museum. "Terrific exhibit," he said, nodding. "That one right there is my favorite." He motioned toward the giant rag doll Jesus sprawled on the floor. The artist had used brown yarn for hair, a heavy black thread to stitch two Xs for eyes. A pair of scuffed boxing gloves were fitted over the hands.

"What's going on here, Carlos?" Ms. Otto's eyes darted to me, to the man walking away, to me again, to the puddle on the floor, then back to me. There was something accusatory about her gaze.

"He did it!" I said, pointing at the man, who was now walking leisurely toward the exit.

"Sir," she called out. "Sir, come back here!" The automatic sliding doors glided open, and the man stepped outside into the bright sunlight. Ms. Otto made a grunting noise like there was a bear inside her throat as she headed

toward the front desk, her bob quivering with each step.

"I told him he couldn't do that," I said to her back.

Ms. Otto began questioning the receptionist, who lifted the handset of the telephone and turned in my direction. I held my hands out and shook my head slowly as if to say, *There wasn't anything I could've done to stop that man from urinating.*

Ms. Otto stormed off, furious, her heels echoing throughout the museum.

I put my hand against my jacket pocket where I kept my bag of Red Vines. Now wasn't a good time. I was addicted to the red licorice, its sweet flavor and gummy texture, but it also kept me from biting my fingernails, a nervous habit I had had as far back as I could remember. I was probably biting my nails inside my mother's womb.

Seconds later Ms. Otto returned with a roll of paper towels and an aerosol can. "We're going to have to clean this up." She handed me the paper towels while she sprayed the area with Glade. Now the museum smelled like Tropical Mist *and* urine.

"Do you have any rubber gloves?" I asked her. "And a trash bag?"

"Yes, yes, I'll be right back." She set down the aerosol can and marched off.

I unspooled the paper towels like a giant scroll, tore off about ten sheets, and let them fall on the puddle. I imagined myself in a commercial, testing the durability of one brand of paper towels over another. *What's this?* I heard the narrator say. The camera slowly zoomed to the urine pond on the floor of the museum. *Nothing Brawny can't handle. So strong. So soft.* Then there'd be a shot of me in my museum guard uniform, on my knees, wiping. *That's triple-action performance. That's Brawny.*

Ms. Otto came back with a plastic trash bag and a pair of rubber gloves that were taxicab yellow. "Here you go, Carlos," she said. "I need to make some phone calls. Can you take care of this?"

"Sure," I said, trying to conceal my irritation.

"Great. Thanks," she said, then trotted back to her office.

If someone had told me the week before that in seven

days I would be wearing a navy blue suit and rubber gloves, mopping up another man's piss beside an eight-foot stuffed Jesus wearing boxing gloves, I would've asked him what he was smoking.

"Hey," a voice said from behind me. It was the receptionist. She was about my age and had the same hairstyle as my girlfriend, Mira—straight blond that flipped up at the shoulders. The receptionist's eyes were a dull blue, her nose small and pudgy. Beige freckles spotted her cheekbones.

"Hey," I said back.

"That sucks."

"No kidding." I lifted a clump of wet towels and dropped them into the bag.

She scrunched up her face. "God, it *stinks*."

"It smells worse down here."

"I'm Vanessa, by the way."

"Carlos," I said. "I'd shake your hand, but . . ." I raised my gloved hands.

"Ms. Otto had me call the police," she said. "They should be here soon."

7

"I hope they catch him." I spooled out more towels and wiped again.

"So this is your first day, huh?" she asked.

"Yep."

"It can only get better."

"I hope so."

"You in school?" she wanted to know.

"Junior at Millikan," I said. "You?"

Vanessa smiled. "*I* go to Millikan."

"I don't think I've ever seen you around."

"I just transferred a week ago," she said. "I was at Wilson. Millikan feels a lot bigger. Like I'm in college all of a sudden."

"How come you transferred?"

Her smile dissolved, she dipped her head. "I had some problems with my last school." She crossed her arms and leaned against the wall. "Long story," she said.

I looked up at Vanessa, her shifting eyes.

"So what do you think about all this stuff?" She stepped away to the middle of the museum, her hands at her waist.

"I don't get some of it," I admitted.

"I hear you."

"I mean, I could've done *that*." I pointed at the giant canvas hanging on one wall. It was completely black, as far as I could tell. "That's not painting," I said. "That's covering."

Vanessa walked over to the pink neon sign on the opposite wall. In a script font it read:

No more coitus for you.

The sign buzzed softly like an old refrigerator and turned Vanessa's face pink. She tilted her head to one side. "I kinda like this one," she said.

"Me too," I agreed.

The phone at the front desk began ringing, and Vanessa hurried off. "Nice meeting you, Carlos."

I lifted my gloved hand. "Same here."

I finished cleaning up and cinched the trash bag closed, then sprayed some more Tropical Mist around the area. Even though I was wearing rubber gloves, I washed my hands really well in the museum's bathroom before returning to my post. I pulled back my coat sleeve and looked at my watch. I had four hours left in my shift.

Unlike my previous job at Ralph's, bagging groceries and rounding up shopping carts, this was a pretty easy gig. All I had to do was sit on my ass and keep my eyes open. It paid a quarter per hour less, sure, but at least I wasn't pushing a train of carts under the sun or running price checks. Besides, I just needed a little cash flow to fill my gas tank and buy Mira some nice things every now and then. If my mom and Ms. Otto weren't in the same book club, had my name not come up when Ms. Otto mentioned one of her guards quitting without giving her two weeks' notice, I'd probably still be asking strangers, "Paper or plastic?"

An hour or so later a police officer arrived and I told him everything about the man that I could remember. His goatee, his slender nose, his sleepy eyes. "He said the stuffed Jesus was his favorite," I said. The officer glanced at the giant rag doll sprawled on the floor and scratched the side of his face. He flipped through his notes and thanked me for my cooperation. I headed back to my post.

Late in the afternoon a family of four came into the museum. They seemed out of place, disoriented. I expected the father to pull out a tourist map from his back pocket at any minute. He had a belly like a globe and walked around the museum with his hands deep in his pockets, rattling his car keys. His daughter was thirteen, maybe fourteen, listening to her iPod, mouthing the lyrics and bobbing her head slightly while she wandered aimlessly around the room. The mother was heavyset and wore a T-shirt with a cartoon honeybee that had red and blue stripes instead of black and yellow. Above the oblong wings it said: PROUD TO BEE AN AMERICAN. Her son hovered close to her, timid. As they neared the neon sign, the boy said, "Mom, what's coitus?" Except he didn't know how to pronounce the word and added another syllable: co-eye-tis, like it was some kind of disease.

"Oh, it's nothing," the mother said.

"What does it *mean*?" the boy pleaded.

"I don't know."

"Yes you do." He was practically yelling.

The mother looked at me and smiled nervously.

"Come on, Blake. Let's go see Grandpa Joe."

I pushed a fist against my mouth, stifling my laughter, air wheezing out of my nostrils.

Once the family had left, I slipped out my Red Vines and pulled a piece from the ripped corner of the bag. I took a large bite and chewed and chewed, the red licorice sticking to the back of my teeth. I wanted to be home already and out of my uniform and on the phone with Mira. I wanted to tell her about my first day.

The neon sign continued to buzz.

The giant pile of green sand sustained its conical shape.

Jesus the boxer stayed put—knocked out, flat on his back, fragile as anyone.

ISABEL

The one-year anniversary of the death of my boyfriend was approaching and the events of that Monday afternoon were coming back to me, playing in my head like a movie. He'd just dropped me off at home and said he'd call after he left Ferraro's, the Italian restaurant where he bused tables and refilled customers' drinks. He was already dressed in his uniform—black pants, white shirt, red vest. Before he rolled up the car window and sped off down my street, I kissed those full lips of his and tasted the spearmint of his gum.

It happened shortly after, on Studebaker Road, just north of the 22. The eyewitnesses said he was driving way over the speed limit, that he was making a left-hand turn when he lost control of his car. It skidded, jumped the curb, then crashed through a chain-link fence before rolling down into the glittering blue water of the canal.

A few weeks after Gabriel's death I pulled down this ratty dictionary I had in my closet, sandwiched between my junior high yearbook and a stack of CDs, and looked up a word that had been gnawing at me even though I basically knew what it meant:

> **fate** \ˈfāt\ *n* (14c) **1 :** the principle or deter-
> mining cause or will by which things in
> general are believed to come to be as they
> are or events to happen as they do: DES-
> TINY **2 a :** an inevitable and often adverse
> outcome, condition, or end **b :** DISASTER;
> *esp*: DEATH **3** *pl, cap* : the three goddesses

who determine the course of human life
in classical mythology

I sat there on the edge of the bed with the dictionary split open on my lap, looking out my bedroom window at a trio of birds clipped to a TV antenna, little black starlings, until one by one they flew away. I couldn't accept the idea that Gabriel was *destined* to die the way he had, that somehow it was all *inevitable*. If so, if that was how the universe operated, then we are all just theater puppets, moving this way and that way by some invisible hand. It would mean people couldn't be held responsible for their choices. Just blame it on whoever's pulling the strings.

Then I looked up *free will*, skimming forward through the thin and dusty pages, and saw that the definition contradicted *fate*.

Then I looked up *god*.

Then I looked up *death*.

Then *remorse*.

Then *love*.

Then I looked up *Isabel* and was surprised to see it wasn't included even though other names were, but I pictured it there anyway, right there between *Isaac* and *isallobar*.

> **Is·a·bel** \'iz-ə-bel\ *n* (2006) **1 :** a heartbroken teenager from Long Beach, California, whose boyfriend recently died in a car accident **2 :** who is now looking up words like *fate* and *love* in a dictionary because she's hoping to find the meaning of life—or at least a sign— within its yellowing pages **3 :** who now feels that familiar dull ache in her heart as if someone had pushed a thumbtack into it

I was a mess for months—crying in the shower, in bed, during class, at the dinner table—and then I reached a point where I was just going through the motions, a zombie of a girl, my mind elsewhere and nowhere at once. Sometimes I'd be hanging out with Heidi at one of the orange tables in the quad and all of a sudden I'd have tunnel vision. It happened quite often: this sensation that I was looking at the world through a glass tube. Sound was muffled. Everything in slow motion. Then Heidi would nudge me on the arm and say something like, *Earth calling Isabel.* That's what happened yesterday.

"Sorry," I told her. "I don't know what's wrong with me."

Heidi twisted her lips and shook her head. "It has almost been a year, Is." She reached across the table and placed her hand over mine. "You've been thinking about him a lot lately."

I looked across the quad at some kids leaning against the chain-link fence, a boy with his hands jammed inside his front pockets, his friend on a cell phone.

"Yeah," I sighed.

Heidi gave my hand a little squeeze.

Soon after, Matt Hawkins walked past us wearing his Oakleys and letterman jacket. He pointed at someone he knew by the fence and smiled, the sky reflecting in his lenses.

Heidi raised a fist to her mouth and bit down on the second knuckle of her forefinger. "Umph," she grunted.

"He's okay," I said.

"Just *okay*?"

"He's got a big forehead. You can watch a movie on that thing."

"It doesn't bother me so much," Heidi said.

"And why does he wear his letterman jacket all the time? I think he tries too hard."

"But would you do him?" she asked.

"No way."

"I'd do him in a second," she said, grinning.

The thing was, I had a hard time thinking about hooking up with anyone, let alone some big-headed jock in wraparound shades. Whenever I looked at some boy who I thought was cute, whenever I imagined myself with him, even for a second, part of me felt guilty, like I was still with Gabriel and considering cheating on him. It was no surprise that I hadn't dated or kissed anyone since he died.

"You all right?" Heidi asked.

"Yeah," I said unconvincingly.

A girl approached us then with blond hair that curled up at her shoulders. She looked distressed. "You guys mind if I sit here for a second?" she asked. "I think I lost my cell phone."

"Not at all," I said.

"Thanks." She had a small nose and freckles the color of sand. She set her purse down on the table and began rummaging through it. I could hear her keys jingling in there, something plastic clicking against something plastic—a tube of lipstick, a compact, a ballpoint pen. "I need to clean this thing out," she said, flustered, poking around her purse. "Shit. I hope I didn't leave it at the museum."

"What's your number?" Heidi asked, pulling out her own cell phone. The girl told her, and Heidi dialed, her thumb moving quickly over the numbers. She motioned with her eyebrows at another boy, her neck bent slightly. "How about him, Is?" she said.

He was tall, broad-shouldered, with thick curly hair. "He's kinda cute," I said.

Heidi swayed her torso like an exotic dancer. "Oh, I'd do him for sure." She looked at the girl, her phone still to her ear. "It's ringing," she said.

The girl tipped her head toward her purse. Silence. "I knew it," she said. "I must've left it at work."

"Hello? Who's this?" Heidi said to the person on the other line. She handed the girl her phone. "It's Mr. Ziolkowski," she said, her mouth twisted downward in disgust.

The girl lifted Heidi's phone to her ear. "Hi, it's Vanessa from second period," she said. "Sorry, sorry . . . Where are you now? . . . Okay, I'll be right over. . . ." She hung up and handed the phone back to Heidi. "Thank you," she said, rising up from the table.

"No problem."

"Where's the teachers' lounge?" she asked. "I'm sort of new here. Just point me in the right direction."

I looked at Heidi. "Let's show her."

Heidi stood up from the table. "Come on, let's go."

"Thanks, guys. I'm Vanessa, by the way."

"I'm Heidi."

"I'm Isabel," I said. "You can call me Is."

"Okay, Is," she said.

I liked Vanessa immediately. I could tell she wasn't a snob. She seemed sweet, down-to-earth, maybe a little shy. Her voice had a lilt to it that made it sound like she was always asking a question. She wore a cute green top with stonewashed jeans and had this shiny silver bracelet with black stones in it like drops of ink.

"Thanks," she said when I told her how pretty it was. She lifted her arm and rotated her fist back and forth like she was trying to open a door. Her bracelet flashed in the sunlight. "My mom bought it for me for my birthday."

"I wouldn't trust my mom to buy me anything," Heidi said. "She wears the ugliest jewelry."

It was true. All the times I'd seen Heidi's mom in person she was wearing these godawful earrings. One pair was gold and looked like flattened bottle caps. One had feathers that dangled from big hoops. *Feathers!* I wondered what she would hang from her ears at a funeral, what hideous stones she had to go with a black dress. Then I wondered who the funeral was for, who was lying inside the casket.

That was something else I'd been doing more often, along with the tunnel vision: thinking about death. When my mom told me the other day I had a face like a cherub, I asked her, *What's a cherub?* and she said, *A child with wings, an angel child.* I said, *So a cherub is some kid that died.* And she said, *Well, in a sense, yes.* She walked away and then I started thinking about all the kids dying at that moment around the world and becoming cherubs, wings sprouting from their shoulder blades. A boy falling off a roof. A girl snatched off the street. A boy in a hospital gown with a bald head. A girl on a crosswalk, oblivious, a truck barreling down on her. Dreamlike, morbid visions.

Issues. I had them. So sue me.

Heidi turned to Vanessa before we entered the administration building, a one-story structure with stucco walls and gray doors, very bleak. "You know about Mr. Ziolkowski, right?"

"Nuh-uh," Vanessa said.

We stopped walking.

"What?" she said. "Tell me."

"Mr. Z's a *total* perv," Heidi said. "Haven't you noticed

how he looks at some of his students? The girls *and* the boys?"

Vanessa nodded repeatedly. "Yeah, there's definitely something creepy about him."

"Miranda Brewer told me she saw him on 4th Street wearing a dress," I said.

Vanessa's eyebrows jumped up her forehead. "Shut. Up."

"Her boyfriend saw him, too," Heidi added.

"We had a teacher like that at Wilson."

Heidi and I waited to hear more, both of us looking at Vanessa intently. She turned her head toward the parking lot as if she'd heard someone calling her name. "Yeah," she said, even though neither Heidi or me asked her a question.

We went into the administration building, down the west hallway, and found Mr. Z sitting on a coffee-colored sofa chair, his long legs stretched out and crossed at the ankles. You could tell he was as tall as a streetlamp even though he was sitting down. He was thin, bird-faced, with short blond hair that bristled on the top of his head like a toothbrush. He reminded me of a skeleton, which reminded me of death, which made me wonder when he was going to die, where and how, and then I imagined him keeling over in the grocery store, his body crashing into a pyramid of apples, thumping like red fists on the waxed floor before wobbling away from him.

"I'm so sorry, Mr. Z," Vanessa said.

He reached into his shirt pocket and slipped out Vanessa's phone. It looked ridiculously small in his hand, like a Matchbox car or a nine-volt battery.

"These things are constantly ringing in my class," Mr. Z said. His voice cracked a bit like he was in the middle of puberty. "If your phone ever rings during my class, it's automatic detention."

"It won't," Vanessa said. "I promise."

"Good," he said. He extended his long, bony arm and handed Vanessa's phone back to her. When Mr. Z stood up I thought his head was going to punch right through the ceiling. "See you tomorrow," he said, and headed out the double doors, taking languid, ostrichlike steps.

When Mr. Z was gone, Heidi asked Vanessa if she'd

ever played Who Would You Do?

"How do you play it?" Vanessa said.

"It's not really much of a game," I told her.

"Would you ever jump on Mr. Z's bones?" Heidi asked point-blank.

Vanessa had this I-just-sank-my-teeth-into-an-icy-lemon-wedge look on her face. *"Never,"* she said.

Heidi grinned. "That's how you play."

"I told you it wasn't really much of a game," I said.

Vanessa looked at Heidi. "Would *you?*"

"Never," she said. "But I bet he has a nice, long salami."

Vanessa covered her mouth with her hand. "Oh God, don't make me think about Mr. Z's dick!"

Heidi and I started to laugh.

And just like that the three of us became, well, the three of us.

CARLOS

Me and Snake were kicking it on the bleachers, roasting in the sun, instead of sitting in biology and learning something we'd probably forget in a year anyway. It was February, but it felt like summer, felt like you could fry an egg on my forehead. The air above the blacktop rippled in the heat where freshmen in PE tossed a basketball up and down the courts. Their bodies rippled too, their scrawny arms and legs, like a television with bad reception.

Snake let out a guttural burp. I glanced at my watch. We were waiting for Will and Suji, his girlfriend. We all planned to ditch our last three classes and head out to the beach. *Meet us by the basketball courts,* I'd told them. I had asked Mira to come along, but she had a test in history she couldn't miss. *We can go to the beach this weekend,* she finally said. *I have to work at the museum,* I reminded her. A continuous flow of students moved around us like a river coming to a boulder, splitting, then braiding together again. *We'll think of something,* she said, and hurried off in the opposite direction, but not before she pecked me on the lips, softly, like a raindrop had landed on my mouth.

We met at a beach party last summer, Mira and I. There were twenty or so people, including Will and Snake. There was an ice chest sunk into the sand stocked with beer and Sparks, with peach and peppermint schnapps. A bonfire made our skin golden, an ocean crashed and shushed in the darkness behind us.

I saw her on the other side of the flames, sipping from a bottle and chatting with a friend. I recognized her immediately. She was that mysterious girl I spotted every now and then walking by herself across the quad, shy and beautiful, always in a hurry, as if she was late for an appointment. Someone leveled the sand with his palm and laid a beach blanket across it, then twirled an empty beer bottle over the striped fabric. A small group gathered, excited to play, and I was surprised to see that the shy girl had scooted up to the blanket. Snake was wasted, flicking his tongue between his parted fingers, smashed against his lips. *Can we kiss anywhere?* he asked. We were all pretty drunk. The ocean boomed, the gold light of the bonfire pulsed over our skin, and a few spins of the bottle later, Mira and I brought our lips together.

We began dating that summer, kissed some more and messed around, her shyness slowly dissolving over the months like an ice sculpture as she became more confident, less meek—a different person altogether.

"Where the hell are they?" Snake asked.

"They'll be here," I said.

"Hey, man, did you hear about those puppies?" Snake was drawing abstract flames with a Bic on the side of his red Converse.

"What puppies?"

"The drug puppies."

"Nuh-uh."

"These drug smugglers cut open their bellies and slipped some packets of heroin inside them," Snake said, now drawing on the other side of his shoe. "Then they stitched them back up."

"That's some evil shit right there," I said.

Sweat glinted on his forehead like bits of glass. "Those drug smugglers are some creative mofos," he said.

"They really know how to think outside the box."

"What will they come up with next?"

Snake capped his pen and we both watched the freshmen run sluggishly up and down the courts, yelling at one another. "Pass the ball, pass the ball!" they shrieked. "Here, over here!" One kid took a shot from the three-point line and the orange Spalding clanged off the rim and out of bounds. "I told you to pass the damn ball!" another kid screamed.

"A dolphin," I said. "They'll train a dolphin to deliver their heroin. In a waterproof vest with lots of pockets."

"Or a carrier pigeon," Snake said.

"A dolphin would carry more dope."

"Not if they had a whole flock of pigeons. Then they could strap little Baggies to each one."

"Good point," I said.

I zipped open my backpack and took out my Red Vines. I pulled a piece from the bag before handing it to Snake. He jammed the licorice into his mouth and gnawed on it.

"Has anyone else pissed in the museum yet?" Snake asked, chewing.

"Nope," I said. "Man, that dude was psycho."

"So all you have to do is sit there and keep an eye on people?"

"Pretty much."

"Sounds boring as shit."

"It's better than working at Ralph's," I said. "I'd rather sit than run around sweating."

"I guess," Snake said. "What time is it?"

I glanced at my watch. "Quarter till one."

"Where the hell are they?"

"Hell if I know."

"They're probably boning."

30

"Probably."

"Which one's her house again?"

I surveyed the track homes that lined one side of the soccer field and pointed. "I think it's that yellow one over there."

Snake wiped the sweat from his forehead with the back of his hand. "Damn sun," he said, looking up, squinting. "Knock it off."

I held the coiled licorice between my teeth and pulled. I wondered if there would ever be a day when I stopped eating Red Vines. I pictured myself ninety, blue-haired with thick bifocals, chewing on the red licorice with my dentures.

"You think they used any anesthesia on the puppies?" Snake said.

"That would be messed up if they didn't."

"It's already messed up."

"I know. I'm just saying it would be even *more* messed up."

"There they are," Snake said. He jerked his chin toward the track homes.

Will had already jumped the wall of brick that separated Suji's house from the school soccer field. She was sitting on top of the wall and Will's hands were lifted up toward her, like he was reaching for a vase on a high shelf, but then she waved him off and jumped down without his help. They crossed the field, Will with his hands in his pockets and Suji with her head down, her long hair shining blue-black in the sun. When she finally lifted her head she gathered a few loose strands away from her face with a hooked finger and slid them behind her ears.

"Hey, Carlos. Hey, Snake," Will said.

"Sorry we're late, you guys," Suji said. "It's my fault."

"You do the hokey-pokey and you turn yourself a-round," Snake sang. He grunted twice, thrusting his hips forward. "That's what it's all a-bout."

We laughed, Snake and I, like hyenas on nitrous. Will and Suji sat down on the bleachers and kept quiet. She turned to face the kids scrambling for the ball on the basketball courts.

"I'm just goofing," Snake mumbled.

Will cleared his throat as if he was going to say something but then started fingering a piece of thread twisting from the corner of his shirt pocket.

"Anyone want a Red Vine?" I offered.

"No thanks," Will said.

Suji shook her head no.

A boy shouted on the courts: "Foul, foul! I was fouled, man!"

Will pinched the corner of his shirt pocket between his thumb and forefinger and lifted it to his mouth, lowering his head at the same time. He held the thread between his front teeth and yanked, then spat the thread out onto the blacktop.

No one was talking. Something had obviously happened between Will and Suji, an argument about something silly, I figured. Me and Mira had been seeing each other for six months and fought only once during that time. I'd caught her checking out some guy on 2nd Street. She said she wasn't and I said she was and suddenly the vibe between us turned black. Next thing I knew she was weeping.

"Did you guys hear about the puppies?" I finally said.

Will looked at me. "What puppies?"

I slapped Snake on the arm with the back of my fingers. "Tell 'em."

"These crazy drug smugglers sliced open some puppies and put heroin inside their bellies," he said.

Suji turned her attention away from the basketball courts and looked at Snake.

"That's got to be a hoax," Will said.

"No, man. I saw it on the news this morning. Matt Lauer and shit."

"Did they die?" Suji wanted to know.

"Some did," Snake said, "but they were able to save three that still had dope in them."

"God, that's awful." Suji turned back to the courts, but her eyes were focused someplace farther. The parking lot. The gleaming cars going up and down Palo Verde. The houses on the other side of Palo Verde. The leafless February trees.

Snake grabbed my backpack and unzipped it.

"What the hell?" I said.

"Getting another Red Vine."

"Why don't you ask, dickhole?"

Snake slipped out a piece and jammed it into the corner of his mouth. "Can I have one?" he said, chewing and grinning like an idiot. "Please, Carlos?"

Will chuckled, and Suji jerked her head in his direction. There was anger blazing in her dark brown eyes.

"So are we going to the beach or are we just going to sit here?" Snake asked.

Will had his head down. "I can't, man. I have a quiz in algebra."

"You just remembered that now?" Snake said, irritated.

A basketball came bouncing toward Suji in short hops. She caught the ball and held it at her midsection, her elbows pointed outward as if she was about to toss it back into the courts. A boy lacquered in sweat came running with his palms out before him.

"Here," he said.

Suji held the ball.

"Come on," he said.

Suji held the ball.

"What's her damn problem?" the boy asked.

ISABEL

Back in September, my dad clipped out a chart from the *Los Angeles Times* and left it on the kitchen counter by the coffeepot. I had just woken up and was moving around the kitchen with the speed of a slug. I took down the box of Cheerios from the top of the fridge, my favorite red bowl from the cupboards, and set them both on the counter. That's when I saw the newspaper clipping. The chart was labeled "Risk of Death" and looked like this:

Risk of Death

This chart lists some causes of death, their annual numbers, and the odds that a U.S. citizen will die of each over the course of his or her lifetime. For example, the lifetime risk of being killed by alcohol poisoning is one in 10,530.

Cause	Annual Deaths	Lifetime Odds
Heart disease	652,486	One in 5
Cancer	553,888	One in 7
Diabetes	71,372	One in 54
Motor vehicles	44,933	One in 84
Homicide	16,137	One in 226
Assault by firearm	11,624	One in 324
Fire or smoke	3,229	One in 1,167
Fall from stairs or steps	1,638	One in 2,301
Airplanes	747	One in 4,858
Drowning in bathtub	402	One in 9,377
Accidental electrocution	376	One in 9,968
Alcohol poisoning	358	One in 10,530
Lightning	46	One in 81,949
Flood	22	One in 171,348
Venomous spider	14	One in 269,262
Fireworks discharge	2	One in 1,884,832

I set the clipping on the kitchen table and opened the box of Cheerios and shook some out into my bowl. I took the milk out from the fridge and tipped the carton, a long white tongue that stretched into the mound of cereal. The coffeepot gurgled and hissed, and suddenly I couldn't help but see it as an appliance that could kill. Within the plastic black shell of the coffeepot, all the components were already in place for an electrocution: the dripping water, the hidden circuit and wires behind the digital clock, the emerald light beside the ON switch. I sat down at the kitchen table with my cereal and tried not to think about it.

My mom came out of the bathroom in her terrycloth robe and fuzzy slippers. "Good morning, Izzy," she said.

"Morning."

"Aren't you late for school?"

"No, not yet."

"Is that milk still good?"

"It seems fine to me," I said, lifting a spoonful of cereal to my mouth.

"You should've checked the expiration date." My mom opened the cupboard and took down her coffee mug with the bright yellow happy face painted on it. Its eyes were two black spirals.

"Who clipped out the chart from the newspaper?" I finally asked her.

"Your father did," she said. "He thought it was interesting."

"Kinda morbid, don't you think?"

"Yes, in a way." My mom reached for the coffeepot and my stomach tightened. "It's also good to know," she said, grabbing the handle and filling her mug.

I picked up the clipping again. "Why's it good to know that one in two hundred and twenty-six will die from homicide? That'll only make you paranoid."

"One in two hundred and twenty-six? Seems a bit high." My mom leaned over my shoulder and I pointed to the figure on the chart. She took a sip from her coffee. "Oh look, the death rate by airplane is seven-forty-seven. Isn't that funny?"

"Hilarious."

My mom bumped me lightly on the arm with her hip.

"You know what I mean."

"But why is it important for me to know that, on average, seven hundred and forty-seven people die annually by airplane?"

"I was thinking more of the heart disease one and cancer." My mom leaned against the kitchen counter with her mug held by her chin. The happy face was freaking me out, its dark eyes and maniacal smile. "Now that I think about it, it's time for my yearly," she said.

I dipped my spoon into my bowl. I'd always thought Cheerios looked like tiny doughnuts, and now I saw them as miniature life preservers. The chart said four hundred and two people drown annually in bathtubs, but didn't list how many drown in oceans or lakes or swimming pools, or in a river channel like Gabriel had. I didn't want to, but I thought of him seatbelted in his submerged car, the bubbles rising from his mouth and his dark hair swaying like some aquatic plant. I felt this twinge in my heart, a pinprick of sadness, and wished more than anything that he was in my life again, on his way to my house so the two of us could drive to school together like we used to. I could imagine him jogging up the walkway now, the morning sun shining on him, car keys jingling in his hand.

Roland, my little brother, came out of his room yawning with a severe case of bedhead. He had this I'm-technically-awake-but-for-all-intents-and-purposes-still-sleeping look on his face.

"Good morning, pumpkin." My mom ruffled his hair as if it needed to be more messy.

"I'm not a pumpkin," he said, rubbing his eyes. "Can you make me some pancakes?"

"Sure, sweetie."

Roland dug into his nose. "I'm not a sweetie."

"That's disgusting," I said. "Use a tissue, why don't you."

My brother shuffled to the kitchen table and reached into my cereal with his little hand, plucking a Cheerio from the bowl.

"Mom!" I hollered.

"What is it?"

"Roland just picked his nose and stuck his hand in my cereal!"

"Stop pestering your sister, Rolo."

"Pancakes, pancakes, pancakes," he mumbled.

"Okay," my mom said. "Hold your horses."

Roland sat down at the table and scratched his head. "I don't have any horses."

The thought that there was maybe a speck of my brother's booger in my Cheerios, however microscopic, made me lose my appetite. I pushed the bowl toward him. "It's yours now," I said.

"I don't want it," he said. "I'm having pancakes." He began drumming his fingers on the tabletop.

"Brat."

"Poophead."

"You were adopted."

"No I wasn't, poophead."

"Ask Mom."

"Mom."

"You weren't adopted," my mom reassured him.

I leaned in close to him. "She's lying," I whispered.

"Your real parents are in North Carolina. And they're both big morons."

My brother stuck his tongue out and crossed his eyes.

"They look *just* like that," I said.

"Okay, you two. *Enough*," my mom scolded.

She placed my brother's frozen pancakes in the microwave and pushed a few chirping buttons. The microwave hummed, the window glowed a muted yellow, and I wondered about death by exposure to radiation, which was also missing from the "Risk of Death" chart. I realized there were lots of ways to die that weren't included. AIDS. Earthquake. Mauling. Ebola. Killer bees. Drowning in a canal while seatbelted in a car.

My dad hurried into the kitchen dressed in his suit and tie, his shiny black shoes, carrying a leather briefcase. I didn't quite understand what he did for work. Something with computers. One Saturday afternoon I sat beside him on the couch while he clicked away on his laptop, plugging numbers into a grid. I'd asked him what he was doing and he said something about "historical data" and "market

44

averages" and other things that went over my head.

"I'm running late," my dad said, pecking my mom on the lips. My dad kissed the top of my head like he always did and then Roland's. "Bye, you guys."

"Bye, Pops," I said.

"Take a banana," my mom said over her shoulder as she buttered Roland's pancakes.

My dad reached into the fruit bowl and twisted one from the bunch. He stepped out into the garage, leaving the musky scent of his cologne behind.

The garage door rumbled open. He started the engine of his car. I shouldn't have looked at the chart again, but I did anyway: 44,933 motor vehicle deaths per year. If Gabriel hadn't been speeding on that day, if he was still alive and actually coming up the walkway at that moment— sunlit, car keys in one hand, the other reaching for the doorbell—would the chart have read 44,932 instead?

I swiped the clipping from the kitchen table on the way to my room and crumbled it up in my hand. There was this knot in my throat, a ball of ache, and when I jumped in the shower I cried under the warm jets of water.

I went to school. I floated from classroom to classroom, hung out with Heidi and Vanessa, and tried not to think of Gabriel, of the chart, of all the ways a person could leave this world.

Later that night my dad came home from work with his jacket draped over his arm and his tie loose, hanging like a stethoscope from his neck. I was happy to see him. Happier than usual, I mean.

Once inside my bedroom, I reached into the wire wastebasket and pulled out the clipping I'd thrown away. I flattened it out on my desk as best as I could, ironing over the numbers with my palm before folding it up and putting it inside my purse.

CARLOS

It was a Tuesday morning when flakes of ash began drifting down. A brush fire was burning out of control in Anaheim Hills and the sky to the east was orange like the light inside a jack-o'-lantern. I passed a driveway where a car was parked, dusted with ash. On the hood was a child's handprint, fingers splayed out like sunrays.

When I got to Millikan, Will stopped me in the hallway. He had this dire look on his face like he'd just run over someone and was now going to ask me to be his alibi. "You got a minute?" he said.

"Yeah, man," I said. "What's going on?"

Will gazed at the floor, half of his hands stuffed in his pockets, his thumbs pointed at each other. He looked up at me, then down again. He slowly shook his head.

"Spit it out," I said.

"It's Suji," he said.

"Did you guys break up?"

He shook his head.

"What is it?"

He lifted his head. "She's pregnant."

"Oh," I said. "Shit, man."

"I know," he said.

A kid on a skateboard rolled behind Will and down the hallway, weaving around students. A girl laughed somewhere, another squealed "Wait! Wait!" as if she were chasing down a bus. Through the open doors at the end of the hallway, I could see an orange strip of sky above the roof of the administration building.

"I'm screwed," Will said.

"What are you going to do?" I asked him.

"She wants an abortion."

"That's probably the best thing."

"It is. I can't be a father now."

"I'm sure Suji doesn't want to be a mother now either."

"Right," he said. "Look, I need to ask you a favor."

"Anything," I said.

Will looked down at the floor again. "Suji doesn't want to ask her parents for the money. And I can't ask my pops because he's an asshole."

Now it was my turn to gaze at the floor.

"I would ask Snake," he continued, "but he doesn't work either." Will's eyes started to water. He looked down the hall, at the otherworldly sky. He bit the inside of his cheek. "I know you just started working at that museum," he said.

"I'm not making much there," I told him.

"I don't know who else to ask. I thought about asking my uncle, but I think he'll snitch on me."

I imagined a hole opening under my feet, my body dropping through it. Part of me wanted to help Will, but another part wished he'd asked someone else. Anyone else.

"I don't know, man," I said, which was the wrong thing to say, I guess, because Will cleared his throat and sniffled and then walked away. *"Will!"* I shouted. But he just kept walking, down the hallway and out the doors and into the orange light.

During lunch, Will was nowhere to be found. It was just me and Snake hanging out by the fences and watching ash tumble from the sky like fish food.

"Where the hell's Will?" Snake asked.

"I don't know," I said.

"And Mira?"

I shrugged.

"Maybe Will's tagging your woman?"

"Eat smegma."

"What's smegma?"

"It's that thing you spread on a cracker before you eat it."

"Man, just tell me," he said.

I saw Mira across the quad, talking to some guy on the track team. She had her arms crossed. He reached into his back pocket and held a note toward her, but Mira kept her arms folded. They stood frozen like that while students moved around them, lugging their books and backpacks. Snake was talking to me, but I wasn't paying any attention. A flake landed on my eyelash. Mira unfolded her arms and took the note from his hand.

I left Snake leaning by himself on the fence and made my way across the quad, students cutting in front of me from the left, the right. Two gulls fought on top of an empty table for a bag of potato chips, pecking and squawking and flapping their gray wings. By the time I reached Mira, the other guy was gone, the note was open in her hands. It was a long letter. So much ink it had to mean trouble.

"What's going on?" I asked her.

"Nothing, it's nothing," she said, forcing a smile.

"Who was that guy?"

"No one. Just someone in my class." Her voice was shaking.

"Mira," I said flatly.

"What?" she said, her eyes tearing up.

We stood there for a while, not talking, not moving,

like two mannequins in a showroom.

"Are you screwing that guy?" I asked her.

She lowered her head.

"Answer me."

Ash swirled around us, the sun burned orange above the cafeteria.

"I'm sorry, Carlos," she finally said. "I'm so sorry."

After school I had to put on my suit and tie and get to work, which was probably a good thing since it kept me from wallowing in my room.

On the drive to work someone honked at me at an intersection. The light was green, but I was just sitting there behind the crosswalk with my foot on the brake. I looked up at my rearview mirror and saw that the driver behind me was scowling, his face tight as a fist.

The daytime guard, Leonard, was sitting at my post when I got to the museum. Leonard was the coolest guy I ever met, which made me feel like a dork around him. He was in his mid-thirties, dark-skinned, his hair clipped close to his scalp. Leonard's movements and speech were fluid and confident. Suddenly the way I walked was too stiff, too awkward, and everything I said was obvious. I imagined he had three or four girlfriends, that he wouldn't care if one decided to leave him for another man.

"What's shakin', Carlos?" he asked.

"Nothing much," I said. I didn't want to get into it, although Leonard was the type of guy who could probably give me some good advice.

He stood up and waved his hand over the folding chair, then he did this thing with his foot like he was slipping on an imaginary banana. "It's all yours," he said. "I kept it nice and warm for you."

"Thanks, man."

He left the museum humming to himself, some ballad I didn't recognize.

I sat down on the chair and let out a big sigh. I reached into my coat pocket and took out my Red Vines. I ate one, then another, then a third. I thought about Mira, how she crumbled when I confronted her. I thought about Will asking me for money, the desperation in his face. I thought about Mira again, saying, *I'm sorry, Carlos. I'm so sorry*. I thought about the potato chips scattering across the tabletop as one of the seagulls took flight, an empty bag pinched in its beak.

I leaned back on my chair and placed my head against the wall even though I wasn't supposed to.

The phone rang at the front desk, but no one was there to pick it up. Ms. Otto came clattering on her heels to answer it, but when she lifted the receiver the caller was already gone. She grunted and slammed the phone down on its cradle and headed back to her office.

I noticed that the pink neon sign hanging on the wall was busted. It flickered from this:

No more coitus for you.

to this:

No more   us for you.

The pitch of the sign's buzzing was a few octaves lower and sounded like a bumblebee trapped inside a jar.

The phone rang again, and again Ms. Otto hurried to answer it. She said a few words to whoever it was on the other line and then hung up. She turned to me and put her hand on her waist. "Where's Bridget?"

"I don't know," I said. "I don't know who she is."

"She's supposed to be working at the front."

"Does Vanessa work later today?" I asked.

"I have her scheduled for tomorrow." Ms. Otto walked toward me. "You know, if there's no one visiting the museum, you can walk around if you want. Stretch out your legs. You don't have to stay in that chair."

"Thanks, Ms. Otto." I pointed at the neon sign. "It's broken."

"I know," she said, frowning. "The artist is coming by to pick it up."

I stood and cracked my back, bending like a yoga instructor.

"I never asked you what you thought about the exhibit," Ms. Otto said.

"It's nice," I said, glancing around the room. "Very modern." What I was really thinking was, *Since when is a pile of green sand art?*

Ms. Otto turned on her heels. "I have to make some calls. Feel free to walk around."

"I will," I said.

I ate one more Red Vine and checked out the pieces up close.

I walked over to the neon sign first, my skin and suit blushing in its pink light. I tapped on the glass tube and it sputtered off and on.

The stuffed Jesus on the floor had me daydreaming about knocking out the other guy, the one who handed Mira the note. I pictured myself walking up behind him, calling him a chump, and once he turned around—*Bam!* Right on the mouth.

I moved over to the pile of bright green sand. It was waist-high and illuminated by a light fixture angled from the ceiling. There was a red square of tape that surrounded the sand, a line that visitors weren't allowed to cross. I walked up to the line and my shadow draped across the green mound. For a long time I stood there, thinking. About Mira, about Will. Along the edges of my shadow the sand appeared to shine a brighter green. I decided then that I would help Will with my first paycheck, and then I changed my mind before changing it again, and then I hovered somewhere between both options—help Will, not help Will—so I wouldn't have to make a decision.

I skipped the large black canvas and headed over to the east wing of the museum. What first caught my attention was a museum guard sleeping in the corner. His hands were folded on his lap, his chest rising and falling under his tie. He wore a dark blue hat like a policeman's, tipped forward, so his eyes were shielded. I thought it was strange that he wore a hat when I didn't have to, that his uniform was different from mine, a lighter shade of blue, with gold buttons down the jacket. My buttons were silver.

There were twin televisions on the floor that faced each other, sitting on DVD players. On one screen was a close-up of a man's face, cropped from the bridge of his nose to the bottom of his chin. He was unshaven, a tiny scar was etched on his cheek like a fingernail's impression. The man whispered, *My starling. Come back. The key is under the doormat.* The video ran for a few seconds more without the man saying anything before it looped again with his plea. On the other screen, a barrage of images flashed like a shuffled deck of cards: [Back of a woman's head] [Empty chair] [Green dress flapping on a clothesline] [Baggage carousel] [Back of a woman's head] [Plane taking off] [Hairbrush] [Unmade bed] [Back of a woman's head] [Rolling suitcase] [Vase of flowers] [Doorknob turning] [Back of a woman's head].

Next I checked out a giant portrait that was made entirely from wads of bubble gum. According to the plaque beside it, the artist used spearmint, grape, banana, strawberry, and Bazooka Joe. I thought about what I could make with a hundred bags of Red Vines, what sort of landscape in licorice.

Soon after, I noticed the empty chair in the corner of the room. It was the same type of folding chair I had at my post. Dark gray, double-hinged, contoured back. I looked again at the museum guard sleeping at the opposite corner. I was confused. Was the empty chair part of the exhibit? Or did the east wing have two guards looking after the same room? I walked over to the folding chair.

There was no plaque on the wall nearby to identify it as a work of art.

"You taking over my shift?" a woman's voice said from behind me.

I turned around. She was roughly my height and wore the same uniform as I did. She was in her mid-thirties, with glasses and thin lips, her brown hair pulled into a ponytail. "No, I'm not," I said. "I'm in the west wing."

"You want to switch posts?"

"No, I was just looking around," I said. "Hey, why are there two guards for this room?"

She laughed.

"What's so funny?"

"Why don't you go over there and introduce yourself?" She pointed at the man sleeping in the corner.

"I don't want to wake him up," I said.

"Just go over there and say hello. Trust me."

I looked at the sleeping guard, his chest moving slowly under his tie, and began walking toward him. The floorboards squeaked beneath my shoes. *Why is she having me do this?* I wondered. And just when I thought I was about to startle the guard awake, I saw what he actually was—a sculpture made from mannequin parts and thrift-store clothing. A whirring sound like a fan came from somewhere within his chest. I crouched and saw that underneath the chair was a motor that made his chest move, a black box with wires rising through a hole cut into the seat. His eyes were painted open on his plastic face. I thought, *He's awake* and *sleeping*.

"What a trip," I said, standing up. "I totally thought he was real."

"It freaks me out," the woman said.

"I keep expecting him to wake up and start moving around."

"You want to switch posts?" she asked again. "I'm sure Ms. Otto won't mind."

"Sorry, but I like where I'm at."

"I don't blame you. It's not bad enough with the creepy guard, I also have to listen to *that* stupid video all day."

We both looked at the televisions on the floor.

My starling. Come back. The key is under the doormat.

"It's so irritating," she said. "No wonder she left him.

I'm Nadine, by the way." She tapped her name tag.

"Carlos," I said.

"Are you new here?"

"I just started last week."

Ms. Otto came around the corner with a sheet of paper in one hand and Scotch tape in the other. "Carlos, I need to step out for a bit," she said. "Richard Spurgeon, the neon sign artist, is going to be here soon to pick up his piece. Would you please put this up after he takes it down?" She handed me the sheet. In all caps it read: REMOVED FOR REPAIRS.

"Sure," I said.

Ms. Otto scurried toward the entrance. When she stepped outside, she swatted the air before her. The hills were still on fire.

"See you later," I told Nadine.

"My starling," she said. "Come back. The key is under the doormat."

I laughed and headed back to my post.

It was a quarter after four. I looked at the sheet and read the words out loud to myself. I thought about the

61

mechanical museum guard in the east wing, just sitting there, dozing away the hours, no ambition, no heart, no pain, which all sounded appealing to me at that moment. I set the sign on the floor and placed the Scotch tape on top of it. With my eyes closed, I leaned back in my chair. I saw the ash sifting down, a child's handprint on the hood of a car. I saw Will walking down the hallway by himself. I saw Mira's face. Her big blue eyes. Her hand rising to her mouth when she turned to leave. My throat felt tight, my chin started to twitch. I was trying to make myself stop crying, which only made it worse.

ISABEL

It was the 7th of February, the one-year anniversary of Gabriel's passing, and I was doing surprisingly okay. Yes, I thought of him and of course I got sad, but it wasn't crippling me like I'd imagined it was going to. It helped that I had Heidi and Vanessa at my side.

The three of us were eating oranges on the couch in the living room. It would've been nice to hang out in the backyard instead, to eat our oranges at the patio table under the big umbrella, but there was too much ash floating around, coating everything with fine white flakes. On the walk home, the air had smelled like burnt cedar. My eyes itched and felt sandpapery.

Heidi dug her fingernail into the navel of her orange, spraying a tiny cloud of mist. Vanessa's orange was already unpeeled, the skin in a mound on the glass coffee table. She thumbed out a wedge and popped it into her mouth. "These are good, Is."

"We have a ton of them." I pointed out the orange tree in the backyard. "Remind me before you leave and I'll grab some for you."

"Thanks."

Heidi rolled her eyes and smirked.

"You too, Heidi," I said, sliding a piece into my mouth.

She nodded and ripped off a chunk of skin.

I got the feeling she felt threatened, like all of a sudden Vanessa would swoop in and become my new best friend.

Vanessa slid her napkin over the coffee table where she'd sprayed the glass with her orange. Last night I'd told her about Gabriel, how he drowned, how much I missed him, and she had listened intently and said all the right things like *Oh, Is, that's so awful, I'm so sorry, I can't even imagine what that was like for you,* her voice a roll of gauze wrapping around a wound. Then she opened up with her own experience with grief, of a childhood friend who'd died of leukemia. It made our bond stronger: A new level of understanding who we were had been revealed. She didn't say much about Wilson and why she transferred to Millikan except that she used to hang out with the wrong crowd. *Drugs and stuff,* she had said. *It got out of hand.* I figured she'd tell me more when she was ready.

Vanessa jerked her head toward the backyard. "Is that your little brother?"

I turned around. Roland was at the edge of the flower beds, crouched and walking sideways with his hands over his kneecaps.

"Unfortunately," I said.

"He's cute."

Heidi coughed, nearly choking on her orange.

"There's nothing cute about him," I assured Vanessa. "Wait till you meet him."

"What's he doing, anyway?" Vanessa asked.

"Trying to catch a lizard," I said. "That's all he does. Watch *SpongeBob* and catch lizards."

"And fart in his hand and lift it to your nose," Heidi added.

Vanessa scrunched up her face.

I stood up from the couch and walked to the sliding glass door. Roland now had the tip of his foot in the flower beds and his hands out as if he were warming them against a fire. I'm not sure when his fascination with lizards began. Last week while he was watching cartoons, I flipped through the journal he was required to keep for Ms. Pritchard, his fourth-grade teacher. Below the dates, he wrote only one sentence to describe each day:

1/30/06
Yesterday I caught 2 Lizards.

1/31/06
Yesterday I was holding a Lizard's tail and it broke off but the tail was still moving.

66

2/1/06
Yesterday I caught a Lizard that was
only big as my pinky.

2/2/06
Yesterday I caught 2 Lizards and 1 didn't
have a tail.

2/3/06
Yesterday I found out Lizards can bite
but it didn't hurt.

In the margins, Ms. Pritchard had written with a red pen:
Oh my, you must have lots of lizards in your yard! Below her
comment, Roland had penciled: *Duh.*

I opened the sliding glass door and the scent of
burning trees blew in. "Don't step on Mom's flowers,"
I told him.

He fluttered his hand behind his back, waving me off.

"She's going to get mad."

"Okay."

Roland lunged at the ground with his hands out, then turned around and tiptoed out of the flower beds with one arm lifted, a thin tail hanging from his fist. I closed the sliding glass door.

"I used to catch grasshoppers when I was a kid," Vanessa said. "God, I was such a tomboy."

Heidi swallowed an orange wedge. "It means you have lesbian tendencies."

Vanessa scowled.

"I'm only teasing," Heidi said. "Don't get your panties in a wad."

I looked at Heidi and opened my eyes bigger as if to say *Be nice,* and she repeated my expression, mocking me.

Vanessa tapped me on the knee. "You need to swing by the museum and meet that guy I told you about. He'd be perfect for you."

"Oh, stop it," I said.

"What about me?" Heidi chirped.

Vanessa turned to her. "You have your Matt 'Massive Forehead' Hawkins."

"He doesn't even know I exist," Heidi whined.

Vanessa turned to me. "I'm serious. Come by."

"Just introduce me at school," I said.

"I *never* see him there. And when I do, you're not around."

"Then it's not meant to be," I said. "I don't like to force things. It just makes the whole thing awkward."

"Oh, Is," Vanessa said, exasperated.

That was the thing with me and Gabriel. It happened naturally. In class, we'd tease each other, he'd bump my elbow while I tried taking notes, I'd poke his side with my pen, then after class, just small talk in the hallway, by the lockers, then serious talk, long conversations about our families, what we loved, what we feared, what we wanted to do when we were done with school, then hands, hands and skin, then kissing and love, then he was gone.

While I was watching Heidi break apart her orange, slipping her thumbnail between two pieces, I had tunnel vision—the world through a glass tube again, the sound turned low—and I pictured the three of us as skeletons. Vanessa lifted an orange wedge with a bony hand to her skull, Heidi's chewed piece slid behind the bars of her rib cage. I wiggled the fingers of my right hand and imagined the tiny bones rattling like dice.

"Is, what's wrong with your hand?" Heidi asked.

I made a fist and stretched out my fingers, again and again. "It fell asleep."

"That's weird," Vanessa said.

"It happens sometimes."

Heidi made a face like she thought I was crazy.

Roland opened the sliding glass door. "Can I bring him inside?" He raised his fist, the lizard's tail dangling from it like a broken rubber band.

"No, Rolo," I said. "Let him go and come meet my friend Vanessa."

"Please."

"I said *no*."

Roland twisted his face and closed his eyes halfway. "*I said no*," he mush-mouthed.

"That's really mature."

"That's really mature," he repeated.

"My name is Roland and my parents are big morons living in North Carolina."

He stepped back from the sliding glass door and slammed it shut, the glass vibrating in its frame.

"My God," Vanessa said, swiveling her head slowly. "He's a little monster."

"At least you don't have to live with him," I told her.

Heidi wiped her mouth with her napkin. "I should probably get going."

Vanessa stood up from the couch. "Same here."

"We should all do something this weekend," I said. "Maybe Shoreline Village."

"I have to work at the museum on Saturday," Vanessa said.

I turned to Heidi. "Let's swing by. Then we can go to Shoreline Village afterward."

"Hopefully Carlos will be working," Vanessa said.

The sliding glass door opened again and Roland flew inside with his palm up, hollering, "Look, look!" He turned his hand over the coffee table and the lizard's tail fell onto the glass, twisting and squirming like a worm.

Vanessa shrieked and covered her mouth. Heidi jumped to her feet, grabbing her purse.

"Roland!" I shouted. "Pick that up right *now* and throw it away!"

He was leaning over the coffee table, watching the tail wriggle side to side up close. "Wait till it stops moving."

"Now."

"Just a *second*."

"I have to go, Is," Heidi said, slipping her purse over her shoulder.

I left Roland by himself in the living room and walked Vanessa and Heidi to the door, apologizing. The sky was still a pumpkin color from the brush fire. At the end of the walkway, Heidi turned around and made the thumb-and-pinkie signal, letting me know she'd call later. I closed the front door and headed back to the living room, fuming. Roland was still hunched over the coffee table. He nudged the lizard's tail with his fingertip.

"Wait till Mom gets home," I said.

Roland shrugged. He pinched the lizard's tail and tossed it outside, then wiped his fingers on his pant leg.

"You're disgusting," I told him.

"You're disgusting." He was doing that mush-mouth thing again.

"My name is Roland and my parents are—"

"Shut up."

"My parents are big—"

"Shut up, shut up!" He pressed his hands over his ears.

"My parents—"

"La la la la la," he chanted, heading into the kitchen.

"Are big morons—"

"I can't hear you. *La la la la*—"

"Living in North Carolina!"

He swerved toward me and began swinging his arms like helicopter blades. I grabbed hold of one of his wrists, then the other, his body jerking as he struggled to break loose. I could feel the narrow bones of his arms twisting in my hands and I thought about all the bones in his body, lashing and jerking, and for a split second I imagined myself dancing with a skeleton.

Roland kicked my shin, hard, and I let go of him. His

face was pink with hate. "I'm telling Mom *and* Dad," he threatened.

"Oh yeah? You know their number in North Carolina?"

He said nothing and stormed off to his room and banged the door shut.

I sat down at the kitchen table and rubbed my shin, wondering what sort of bruise I'd get, what shape of scarlet. I looked outside the window and remembered I'd meant to give Vanessa and Heidi some oranges to take home. The tree slumped with the weight of the fruit at the end of our yard. Orange suns glowing under an orange sky.

CARLOS

The neon-sign artist, Richard Spurgeon, showed up at the museum with a pale yellow blanket folded under his arm. I hoped he didn't notice that I'd been crying, that my eyes were pink and swollen, but then I thought I could blame the brush fire, my allergies, all the ash floating around.

His hair was dyed black and was messy, as if he'd just woken up from a nap outside the museum. He wore a wrinkled white T and jeans, his tennis shoes looked like they were mauled by a mountain lion. There was something about his eyes that reminded me of Will's—not so much the color but how deep-set they were, the arc of his brows. I felt ashamed again for not helping my friend when he'd asked for some money.

"Is Janet around?" Richard asked. It was strange hearing someone call Ms. Otto "Janet." Like if Snake called me "Mr. Delgado."

"She had to step out," I said. "She told me you'd be stopping by." I picked up the REMOVED FOR REPAIRS sign and showed him.

"Shit," he mumbled. "I really wanted to talk to her." He bit his bottom lip and dragged a hand through his hair. "Did she tell you when she'd be back?"

"She didn't."

He laughed. It was the kind of laugh that someone makes when they're really upset. Then he muttered something under his breath that I couldn't make out, some criticism about Ms. Otto's timing.

Richard stood before his neon sign, half of his body radiating pink. The "coit" part of the sign was still sputtering off and on.

"That's my favorite one in the whole exhibit," I told him.

"Thanks." He leaned in close and lightly flicked the glass tube. It clinked like a wineglass.

"Too bad it's doing that," I told him.

"I kind of like that it says 'No more us for you' every now and then. It adds to the piece."

"I thought that, too."

"It's very Duchampian."

"What?"

"Never mind."

Richard crouched down and pulled the black cord from the wall socket and the sign went dark. It was practically illegible without the hot pink light burning inside of it. He touched the glass tube and quickly pulled his hand away as if he'd been stung. "I'll have to wait until this cools down a bit," he said.

"We have rubber gloves somewhere," I offered.

"That's all right," he said, chuckling.

The phone rang at the front desk and Bridget, a half

hour late to work, was now there to pick it up on the first ring. Moments later she slammed the phone back down. The museum had been receiving crank calls and I was starting to wonder if it was the urine guy.

"How long do you think before she comes back?" Richard asked.

"Probably ten, fifteen minutes. She's usually not gone long."

He dropped his blanket to the floor and rolled it up like a sleeping bag. "You don't mind if I kick it here for a while, do you?"

"Not at all," I said. "Ms. Otto might mind, though."

"There's a lot of things Janet minds, if you know what I mean."

At first I didn't have a clue what he was talking about. Then it dawned on me: Something had happened between the two of them. My guess was they used to see each other, that Ms. Otto broke it off. Even the unplugged sign supported my theory.

Richard sprawled on the museum floor, the rolled blanket wedged under his head. His fingers were woven together on his stomach like fat shoelaces. He scanned the ceiling above him, turning his head from side to side. "I love these pipes," he said. "I wish I had them in my loft."

"Where do you live?" I asked.

"Downtown. Not too far from here. Do you know where that Greek restaurant is, right there on Pine?"

I shook my head.

"Well, it's right across from there. They have the best stuffed grape leaves. Ask Janet."

"Okay," I said even though I couldn't imagine having a conversation with Ms. Otto in which I'd ask her who has the best stuffed grape leaves in town. I wasn't even sure what they were. I was sure of one thing, though: Richard and Ms. Otto had definitely been together once. *They have the best stuffed grape leaves. Ask Janet.* What else could that possibly mean?

Richard pulled his fingers apart and laid his hands at his sides so it looked like he was imitating the rag doll Jesus on the other side of the room.

"So how long have you been a museum guard?"

"About a week," I said.

"And all you have to do is sit there?"

"Pretty much," I said. "And make sure no one touches the work or gets too close."

He moved his hands behind his head as if he were about to do some sit-ups.

"Some dude peed on the floor a week ago," I said.

"No shit?" Richard's eyes lit up. "What happened?"

"It was the weirdest thing," I said. "This guy just walked in, unzipped, and started pissing like it was no big deal."

Richard laughed loudly, a booming sound that cannonballed from his throat. He clapped his hands once over his head. "Oh, man, that's *good*."

"I think he was nuts."

Richard wiped his eyes. "Maybe he was a disgruntled artist."

"Maybe."

"Or one of Janet's exes."

"Huh?"

"Forget I said that." He cleared his throat. "Where did he do it?"

I pointed. "Right over there, about ten feet from the sand pile."

"That's wild, man."

"My first day on the job, too."

"I'm Richard, by the way."

"I know who you are," I said. "I'm Carlos."

"That's my father's name."

I didn't know how to respond to that, so I just nodded.

"You in school?"

"Yeah. Millikan."

"Really? That's where I went." He sat up. "Say, does Ms. Howe still teach English there?"

"I don't think so."

"She was pretty hot. My best friend was banging her for a while. Like Mary Kay Letourneau."

"I don't know who that is."

"Some teacher who hooked up with one of her

81

students and got pregnant. He was only thirteen or four-teen."

I opened my eyes wide.

"I know," he said. "You've got a girlfriend?"

"I did until this afternoon," I said. I placed my elbows on my knees and leaned forward. My throat felt tight again. I must've done something strange with my face because Richard sat up.

"I'm sorry, man," he said. "What happened?"

"Long story," I said, even though it wasn't. The story was short and simple. It could've been a children's book. Boy meets girl. Another boy meets girl. A taller boy, a more popular boy, a boy with dimples and perfect white teeth. A boy I couldn't compete with.

Richard stood up. "I hear you," he said. "Whatever happened, you'll get through it."

I didn't want to say anything. I was afraid my voice would crack.

"Eventually it'll stop hurting." With one finger he touched the neon sign—cautiously, again and again—as if he were pressing on a piano key.

"Still too hot?" I asked.

"Not really," he said. "Want to help me take this down?"

"Sure."

I got up from my post and took off my jacket and hung it over the chair. Richard unfolded the blanket across the museum floor so it lay directly under the sign. I stood on one end, Richard on the other.

"Just lift it off the hooks," he said. "Hold it by the frame, not the glass tubes."

"I don't want to break it," I said.

"You won't break it. Okay, on the count of three—"

"*Wait*. Is it heavy?"

"Not really."

I blew on my hands. Richard counted down to three. I held my breath and together we lifted the sign off the wall and turned it on its back, carefully placing it on top of the blanket.

"There," Richard said. "How easy was that?"

"Piece of cake."

"Now help me take it to my car."

"Hold on a second," I said. "I just realized something."

"What?"

I squinted. "What if you're not Richard Spurgeon?"

He laughed.

"And you're some guy trying to steal his piece. Some disgruntled artist, like you said."

He continued to laugh.

"Ms. Otto didn't tell me what you look like. Or rather, what Richard Spurgeon looks like."

"Are you serious?"

I crossed my arms.

He reached into his back pocket and slipped out his wallet. It was brown leather and severely tattered like his shoes. He pulled out a business card and handed it to me:

RICHARD SPURGEON
MULTIMEDIA ARTIST
555.439.2161

"Okay, so you're him," I said. I held the card out for him.

"Keep it. I've got a ton of those."

Richard folded the blanket over the sign on all four sides until it was completely covered. I rolled up my sleeves. We faced each other on opposite ends and bent our knees until we were sitting on the heels of our feet. Again, on the count of three, we lifted the sign. We headed toward the exit, Richard walking backward, looking over his shoulder.

"I shouldn't be doing this," I told him. "I'm supposed to look after the pieces, not *carry* them."

"I really appreciate it," he said.

Once we were outside, I was reminded again that acres of trees were still burning. The whole city smelled like a giant ashtray.

"When are they going to put that thing out?" Richard said.

We headed toward the parking lot, my arms straining a bit from the weight of the sign, but I pretended it weighed nothing. Ash whirled silently across the blacktop. We had reached Richard's car, a blue hatchback, when a speck of ash flew into my eye.

"Shit, shit," I said, blinking furiously.

"You okay?"

"I got ash in my eye."

"Hold on." With one hand he fished for his keys in his pocket while the other held the teetering sign.

"Hurry," I pleaded. It felt like someone was scraping my eye with a toothpick.

Richard opened the back door and maneuvered the sign in. Once my hands were free, I rubbed my right eye with a knuckle, trying to massage the ash out of it.

"Sonofabitch," I mumbled.

A silver two-door pulled into the parking lot and a young couple stepped out. They held hands as they walked leisurely toward the pathway that curved around to the entrance of the museum.

"I've got to get back," I told Richard.

"Carlos," he said, "I owe you one, man."

We shook hands and I jogged quickly back to my post, rubbing my eye with the heel of my palm.

The young couple meandered to the east wing of the museum, allowing me enough time to tape up the REMOVED FOR REPAIRS sign. I placed it right between the two metal hooks fastened to the wall. I rolled down my sleeves, slipped on my jacket, and sat back down on my chair before the couple entered the room. They split apart to view the pieces on their own—the woman walking clockwise around the museum, the man counterclockwise. I felt that tightening sensation in my throat again. Mira. How could she do it? How could she cheat on me? And how stupid was I to not even notice that something was wrong with the picture?

The young man moved toward the sign on the wall, his hands behind his back as if he were cuffed. He tilted his head slightly to one side and moved closer, examining the silver hooks secured to the wall, then stepped back, taking in the whole thing. He scratched his chin and crossed his arms and tilted his head the other way.

I didn't know whether to laugh at his mistake or feel sorry for him.

ISABEL

I don't believe in fate, but every now and then something would happen in my life and I'd start to wonder if someone was working behind the scenes, coaxing me toward a certain direction.

One time, long before I met Gabriel, I was daydreaming in my room about Dustin Prewitt, thinking about his big brown eyes, how he tapped his bottom lip with the eraser-end of his pencil in geometry class when he was mulling over a problem, and then the phone rang and a man on the end of the line asked, *Is Dustin there?* Now what were the chances of *that* happening? So naturally I thought we were meant for each other, Dustin and I, even though we hadn't had a real conversation up to that point. Once, I'd asked him if the pencil sharpener was broken and he'd said *yes*.

But then, a couple weeks later, I found out that Dustin was gay, so I went back to not believing in fate again.

Another time I lost my favorite earrings, these silver sunflowers that I bought on 2nd Street, and practically ransacked my room looking for them. I checked my purse, my jewelry box, the nightstand, my backpack, under my bed, all four drawers of my dresser, even behind my dresser, the pockets of anything with pockets hanging inside the closet, my purse and jewelry box again. Nothing. *Come on, Is*, Heidi yelled from the foyer. *The movie starts at five.* And, wouldn't you know it, while we were in line to get our tickets, the girl in front of us was wearing those same *exact* sunflower earrings. Yellow topaz, silver petals. I stood there in awe, looking at the earrings, and had this weird sensation that my entire life had already been lived.

Then there is the time I'm going to tell you about now.

Heidi picked me up on Saturday afternoon in her red Volkswagen Beetle and we headed toward the museum where Vanessa worked. I could tell Heidi didn't want to go. It was all there in the way she changed lanes, how she leaned forward and then fell back in her seat.

We were on Ocean Boulevard—driving and stopping, driving and stopping—with the fancy houses on our right and the sun-dazzled Pacific on our left. Heidi honked, huffed, sighed.

"What's with all this damn traffic?" she said.

"Can you imagine living here?" I was looking out the passenger window at a house with a perfect manicured lawn. It had a three-tiered fountain, a giant bay window, and a balcony on the second floor with two wicker chairs pointed at the ocean.

"When I'm older, this is where I want to live." Heidi readjusted her rearview mirror. "With my husband," she added.

"Who's it going to be this week?" I asked.

"Matt Hawkins. Obviously."

"Ick," I said.

On the sidewalk, a large black dog was pulling a girl with his leash like a motorboat towing a water skier.

"We'd have three or four children, me and Matt," Heidi said.

"Yeah, and they'd all have colossal foreheads."

"Ah, that's *mean*," Heidi said, chuckling.

We were both sort of laughing and then we fell silent for a while.

And then Gabriel's face came to my mind, his dark brown eyes and olivey skin, the little curved scar above his eyebrow where he'd hit his head against a low-hanging ladder in the garage. I was on the phone with him when it happened, I heard the banging and the cell hitting the concrete and a scream leaping out of his mouth. I wondered what sort of sounds he made when his car hopped the curb, if he cursed or yelled when he crashed through the fence and rolled into the canal.

We drove by the last extravagant house with an ocean view and came upon old apartment buildings and newly painted condos. There were beach towels folded over balcony railings, potted ferns and barbecue grills. An old man in a wifebeater, smoking a cigar, watching the waves.

Another traffic light turned red before we could roll through it and Heidi hit the brakes.

"Where did she say the museum was?" she asked.

"On Alamitos. I know where it's at."

"I bet you do," she mumbled.

I looked at Heidi. "What's that supposed to mean?"

Heidi turned to me and then back to the car in front of her. "You just know where everything's at," she said. "I'm always getting lost, that's all."

I could always tell when Heidi was lying. Her eyebrows would bounce up on her forehead and her movements would become exaggerated. "This traffic is killing me," she said.

"We'll just stop by for a few minutes, say hello, then go to Shoreline, okay?"

The light turned green and we lurched forward. "Okay," she said. "Damn, I need to get some gas."

Two blocks later Heidi pulled into a Shell station. While she was filling up, I went inside the mini-mart to get some bottled water. I opened the fridge's sliding door, shivered, grabbed two Evians, and went to the register.

There were a few people ahead of me in line: a barefoot man with a six-pack of Coors, an old man in a trucker hat, and a woman with a bag of cashews and *People* magazine.

I looked out the window and saw Heidi sliding a squeegee across the windshield of her car, wiping the rubber blade with a brown paper towel after each pass. I don't know why, but I felt sad watching her do that. If she had a boyfriend, I imagined that's one of the things he would've done for her.

While the old man paid for his cigarettes, I looked at the wire rack by the counter. It was full of various bagged nuts, beef jerky, and licorice. Soon as I saw the braided Red Vines licorice through the plastic window, I had a craving. My mouth watered at the thought of chewing one, my teeth sinking into that rubbery sweetness.

The line moved forward and the woman placed her *People* magazine and cashews on the counter. Then she pulled the last bag of Red Vines from the rack. "These too," she said.

Heidi was tightening the gas cap by the time I got back to the car. I twisted open one of the bottles and took a big swallow. I tried not to think of the Red Vines, which only made me think about them more—a long, braided, chewy, sweet, red rope swinging behind my eyes.

Heidi climbed in and stretched the seat belt across her chest. "Did you tell Vanessa that we were coming for sure?"

"Yes, I did."

Heidi started the car.

"We don't have to stay long," I assured her. "It'll be fun."

"Museums aren't fun, Is."

"It's not like we're going to look around. We'll just hang out with Vanessa for a while and then leave."

"*Five* minutes."

"Why're you so cranky?"

Heidi eased the car forward. "Where do I go?"

"Turn right here when you can," I said. "This is Alamitos."

Heidi punched the gas and swerved into the street before the approaching cars could pass her.

"Easy," I said, bracing myself on the door handle.

As long as I'd known Heidi, she was always a careless driver. The last time I looked at the "Risk of Death" chart and saw the lifetime odds for dying in a motor vehicle (One in 84), I pictured Heidi in her Volkswagen Beetle. It was people like her who made that number what it was.

Six blocks later and we were pulling into the parking lot of the Long Beach Contemporary Museum. The white building had clean lines and blue-tinted windows that reflected the buildings on the other side of the street. The concrete pathway to the front entrance snaked through the greenest grass I'd ever seen. In the middle of the lawn was a silver sculpture arcing into the sky. It looked like a whalebone covered in tinfoil.

"What's that supposed to be?" Heidi asked.

"I don't know," I admitted.

"I mean, *really.*"

The glass doors opened and I saw Vanessa talking on the phone behind the curved counter of the front desk. She smiled and raised her finger.

"I'm sorry, but we don't offer field trips at this time. . . . Yes, I'm sure . . ." Vanessa rolled her eyes. "She's not in her office at the moment. . . . Okay, let me put you through." Vanessa pressed a couple buttons and then set the receiver down. "What a condescending *jerk*," she said, shaking her head.

"I would've just hung up," Heidi said.

"Well, I can't do that here. Unless it's a crank call."

"I don't let anyone talk to me that way."

"I told you we'd stop by," I said, wanting to change the subject.

"I wish I could hang out with you guys," she griped.

"What time do you get off?"

"Not until eight," she said.

Heidi swiped a finger across the counter as if she was checking for dust. "Bummer."

Vanessa leaned toward me. "He's here," she whispered. "Carlos."

"You're too much," I said, trying not to smile, and then I was checking out the museum, craning my neck and looking at the artwork. "How long have you worked here?" I asked her.

"Not long. About two months."

Heidi raised a closed fist to her mouth and yawned with great exaggeration like a mime at a kid's birthday party.

The phone rang. "Go ahead and check out the exhibit," Vanessa said before picking up. "Long Beach Contemporary Museum," she said in this sophisticated voice.

I turned to Heidi. "Come on."

Heidi had this I'm-so-bored-already-I-could-slit-my-wrists look on her face as she pushed away from the counter and followed behind me.

The first thing we checked out was this huge rag doll wearing a pair of ratty-looking boxing gloves. His eyes were two Xs, his brown hair was made of yarn. The artist

97

had painted a row of red dots across the forehead.

"Is that supposed to be Jesus?" Heidi asked.

"Looks like him to me."

"If my dad saw that, he'd freak out."

"Mine would probably laugh."

There was a large painting hanging on the wall covered with black paint. Heidi pointed and said, "*That's* art?"

"I guess so. We *are* in an art museum."

"Give me a break."

"There's actually names on it," a voice said from the corner. I turned around. It was the museum guard, a boy about my age wearing a blue suit. His hair was short and wavy brown, his skin the color of butterscotch. I thought he was kind of cute and wondered if he was Carlos, the boy Vanessa wanted me to meet. He motioned toward the painting. "I thought it was just a black canvas too until I looked at it up close the other day."

Heidi and I both walked over to the painting and leaned in. It was true. The names sat on top of the canvas like black lily pads on a black pond.

"Oh yeah, now I see them," Heidi said. "Sergeant Lee . . . Butler."

"They're overlapping," I said. "Captain . . . Gary Eckhart."

"Benjamin . . . Ed . . . something."

"Lance Corporal . . . Adam . . ."

"Captain John . . . Martinez."

"Staff . . . Sergeant Maurice . . ." The last name was illegible, tangled with another's first name.

"Why did he make the names so hard to read?" Heidi wanted to know.

"He probably did it on purpose," I said.

"But *why*?"

I shrugged. "I don't know."

The painting reminded me of my father's electric typewriter that I used to play with when I was a kid. I'd run my fingers over the keys, press my palms down again and again, and the typewriter would pop like caps. When I'd reach the bottom of the page, I'd feed the paper back in and do the same thing—*Pop pop pop!*—typing right over the letters.

It didn't take me long to figure out who all these names painted on the canvas were, what war they all died in, which faraway country. It was another cause of death that was excluded in the "Risk of Death" chart. I figured War was somewhere between Airplanes (747 annual deaths) and Drowning in bathtub (402). But I was just guessing. It could have been more than that for all I knew. That's the impression I got from the painting, anyway.

"Look, a woman." Heidi's finger hovered inches from the canvas. "Sergeant Monique Brown."

"Please, don't touch," the boy said.

Heidi turned around and scowled. "I'm *not*," she snapped.

"Don't you two go to Millikan?" he asked us.

I turned around and faced him. "Yeah."

"I thought you guys looked familiar."

"Where do you hang out?" I asked.

"The bleachers by the basketball courts. Sometimes the fences near the quad."

Once I realized this was Carlos, I started to wonder

if Vanessa had told him about me, if she'd mentioned Gabriel at all. Also, what was it about Carlos that made her think we'd be a good match? I wasn't ready for a boyfriend yet, let alone start dating again.

"Wait," Heidi said. "Aren't you friends with Jeffrey McKenzie?"

He smirked. "I call him Snake."

Heidi nodded. "I know who you are now. I mean, I don't know your name or anything."

"Carlos."

"I'm Heidi. And this is Isabel."

I waved at Carlos and smiled. He was definitely cute.

"Isabel," he said slowly.

I smiled again and pulled some of my hair behind my ear.

"Call her 'Is' for short," Heidi said.

"Isabel's better," Carlos said.

I could feel myself blushing a little.

Vanessa walked into the room all bouncy, her hair swaying at her shoulders. "The phone just won't stop *ringing.*"

"Are these your friends?" Carlos asked.

"They sure are." Vanessa stood at my side and gave me this little, goofy hug. "He's cute, right?" she whispered into my ear.

I shushed her.

"Oh my God, that's *hilarious*," Heidi said. She was pointing at a pink neon sign on the wall that said NO MORE COITUS FOR YOU in this swirly font.

"That's my favorite one," Carlos said. "The artist is a really cool guy too."

The phone rang again at the front desk. "See what I mean?" Vanessa said, hurrying to answer it.

Heidi meandered off to inspect a pile of green sand in the corner and I lingered around the middle of the room, hoping Carlos would talk to me.

Then he did.

"You want a Red Vine?"

Carlos reached into his jacket pocket and slid the bag of licorice out. When he pulled a red braid from the opening, I got this chill on my scalp and arms, and again I felt like my life had already been filmed, that this was fate and everything was already determined. I must've made a strange face or something because Carlos said, "What's wrong?"

"You're going to think this is weird . . ." I said.

Carlos chewed on a Red Vine and nodded for me to go ahead.

"I've been *craving* those the whole way over here."

"I always crave them," he said.

And then he held a coiled piece of licorice out to me like the stem of a flower.

CARLOS

When I got home from work I had zero messages on my answering machine. I took off my jacket, untucked my shirt, loosened my tie, and slipped it over my head like I was removing a noose. I turned on my computer and checked my email. Just some spam with the subject heading that read: *ADD 4 INCHZ TO YR P3N1S IN JUST 1 W33K!*

I leaned back in my chair, feeling sorry for myself, wondering why Mira was going out on me. There had to be a reason, and it didn't take me that long to figure it out. From the beginning, her main complaint about me—the only one, really—was how apathetic I was, how little ambition I had. Most of the time I was content just lounging around the house with her, watching television and munching on pretzel sticks. *Let's get out of here and do something,* she often said. And my response was always the same: *Do what?*

My dad stood in the doorframe and knocked on my door. "You hungry, guy?"

"A little bit," I said.

"Your mother and I are thinking of going to Enrique's."

The thought of hanging out with my parents at a Mexican restaurant on a Saturday night depressed me. I sat on my bed and kicked off my shoes. "I'll just eat something here."

"You sure?"

I nodded.

"Okay, kiddo," he said.

It was obvious he knew that Mira and I had broken up, that I was hurting still, but offering me wisdom on matters of the heart wasn't one of my father's areas of expertise. All he could do was call me "kiddo" and curl his lips inward as if he were trying to swallow his mouth.

I unbuttoned my shirt and shuffled to the kitchen in my wifebeater, socks, and blue slacks. I opened the refrigerator and took out some sliced turkey and French's mustard. I heard my dad in the living room muttering something and my mom responding with, *"¿Por qué?"* Seconds later she was in the kitchen holding her purse and wearing a gray sweater. "You don't want to come with us to Enrique's?" she asked.

I opened the cupboard and took down the loaf of wheat bread. "I don't feel like having Mexican."

"But you love their carne asada."

"You and Dad go. I'm just going to have a sandwich."

She stood beside me. "You want me to make it for you, *mijo?*"

"I've got it, Mom."

She placed her hand on my back. "You haven't heard from her?"

I shook my head no and laid some turkey on a slice of

bread. She didn't know the whole story. I had just told her that we split up and Mira was now seeing someone else, some guy on the track team. I left the part out about her cheating on me.

"She'll regret it," my mom said. "I won't be surprised if she dumps this other guy and asks you to come back."

"It's not going to happen," I said.

"You don't know."

"What if I don't want her back?"

"She's a sweet girl."

I squirted mustard on another slice of bread and spread it evenly with a knife. "That's questionable."

"She is, *mijo*. She was always very courteous and thoughtful. Remember she bought your father and me those nice suede slippers for Christmas? She didn't have to do that."

I exhaled heavily and continued sliding the knife around.

"Maybe you should write her a nice letter or send some flowers?" my mom suggested.

That was it—my breaking point—and I tossed the

knife into the sink. "She was screwing another guy," I finally said.

My mom gulped air as if she'd been holding her breath. "That *tramp*."

I heard the garage door grumbling, the car door opening and slamming shut. "Don't keep Dad waiting," I said. "Go."

"We won't be gone long," she said before dashing to the garage.

I took my sandwich and a Sprite to the couch and channel-surfed. Car bomb in Iraq, *Blind Date*, Hurricane Katrina aftermath, *The Simpsons*. I took a bite, a sip, and flipped to MTV, to Madonna in a skimpy pink suit and heels, stretching out on a ballet floor and slowly gyrating her hips. I finished my sandwich and clicked off the television and went to my room to check my email again. More spam on how to lengthen my penis, this time with an herbal pill that was scientifically proven.

I crashed on my bed and looked at the calendar thumbtacked to the wall. Valentine's was three days away. I opened the drawer to my nightstand and took out the red leather box with Mira's gift inside—a silver bracelet with green stones. I hadn't bothered to keep the receipt since Mira had pointed it out two weeks earlier, told me Valentine's Day was just around the corner, wink-wink. If only I'd known she'd been flirting with someone in her history class, that days later she would swing by his house to pick up his notes on the Battle of Gettysburg and Sherman's March, that minutes later they would kiss and a few minutes after that stumble into his bedroom. If only I'd known, I would've had an extra $48.38 in my checking account.

My cell rang and before I checked to see who it was, I wished it was Mira and then, half a second later, wished that it wasn't. The digital display said SNAKE.

"What're you doing, douchebag?" he said.

"Just kicking it," I said.

"You're going to Christopher's thing tonight, right?"

I faked a yawn. "I'm pretty wiped out."

"Don't give me that shit. You're going. We'll come pick you up."

"We?"

"Will's here."

"Oh," I said, wondering if Will was still angry with me, or disappointed, or whatever it was he felt when he'd walked down the hallway as I was calling his name. "Let me talk to him for a second," I said.

Snake passed the phone to Will. "What's up?"

"Hey, I have the money if you still need it," I told him.

"I don't, but thanks anyway."

"Sorry I didn't say yes when you asked me. I felt like an ass afterward."

"Don't sweat it."

"Don't sweat what?" I heard Snake ask in the background.

"Don't tell him," Will said before passing the phone back.

"Don't tell me what?" Snake asked.

"Nothing," I said.

"Bitch, you better tell me."

"It's none of your business."

"Are you gay or something? Is that why Mira left you?"

"Yes, that's exactly it," I said, but what I was thinking

was this: *Because she was bored out of her mind with me. Because I'm a slacker, an idler, a pair of shoes knotted together and hanging from a telephone wire. Stuck. Swaying in the breeze. Because I don't know what the hell I want.*

"I'll get your ass drunk tonight and get it out of you," Snake said.

"I'm not going."

"Come on," he begged. "There's going to be a lot of honeys there. You know Christopher."

"I'm just going to stay in tonight."

"And mope around like a little bitch?"

"I'm not moping."

"You've been King Mopeyhead for four straight days," he said. "Screw her, man. I'm telling you, the best thing for you to do is get out there and bone another hoochie."

"Sage advice," I said, all sarcastic.

"I'm *serious*."

"Forget it. I'm not going."

Snake palmed the phone and said something to Will I couldn't make out except the words "bitch" and "mope." Will said something back and then Snake removed his hand. "Whatever, douchebag," he said before hanging up.

The following Monday I heard all about Christopher's party, how many people were there, how many girls, how much beer and vodka and tequila, the constant whirring of the blender in the kitchen, how loud the music was thumping from the living room, the bong hits by the swimming pool, the stoned German shepherd wobbling around the yard, and finally the cops that arrived to end it all and send the smashed kids home.

"I was *so* hammered," Snake said, swiveling his head slowly.

"I had the worst hangover," Will added. "Felt like someone was tapping the inside of my skull with a mallet."

It was just the three of us on the bleachers, the day overcast and a breeze playing with our hair, the folds of our shirts. The basketball courts were empty except for a few seagulls milling around like windup toys. A dented soda can seesawed on the blacktop whenever the wind bumped into it.

"Who got the dog lit?" I asked.

"I have no idea, but that shit was funny," Snake said. "He almost fell into the pool."

"Christopher always has the best parties, man," Will said.

"Too bad the cops busted it up."

"Stupid cops." Will hawked a loogie onto the black-top. "Did you see that one with his hand on his gun the whole time? I wanted to smack him. What was he going to do, shoot us?"

"Like Dick Cheney," I said.

Snake turned toward us. "What do you mean?"

"Cheney went quail hunting and accidentally shot his friend in the face," Will said.

Snake chuckled. "Oh man, what a *dick*."

"Dickhole Cheney."

"Did he die?" Snake asked.

"He's in the hospital. He's got buckshot inside his face and neck."

"That must've hurt like hell," I said.

"Like my hangover," Will added. "Man, my head was just *pounding*."

A seagull lifted into the air and the others followed, banking around the parking lot and over the administration building, and I wondered if the followers knew where they were going.

"Where's Suji?" Snake asked.

Will hawked another loogie onto the blacktop and said nothing.

"Did you guys break up, too?"

Will scratched the side of his head. "Something like that."

I looked at Will. His eyes were somewhere on the basketball courts, perhaps on the soda can that rocked silently on the blacktop, flashing its dull light.

Snake leaned back on the bleachers, his elbows resting on the aluminum slat. "What happened?"

"None of your business," Will said coolly.

Snake stretched out his legs, crossing them at the ankles. He was wearing his red Converse with the flames he drew on them with a Bic rising from the white soles.

"Whatever," he said.

The school bell rang, a harsh sound that sent the seagulls back to us, white wings against the charcoal sky. They sailed down and landed on the courts, their heads jerking left and right. One snapped fiercely at another. The bird sprung up, squawked, then landed beside the same gull as if nothing had happened between them.

"I can't wait to graduate and get the hell out of here," Snake said. "I'm sick of Millikan." He uncrossed his legs and stood up. "Milli*can't*, more like."

"I take it you're going to your next class," I said.

"There's some chick I dig that sits next to me. She has blue-ribbon tits."

"I think you should tell her."

"Yeah, right." Snake climbed down the bleachers and lifted his middle finger. "Later, bitches," he said. As he crossed the blacktop, he veered to the right and stomped down on the soda can. It curled around his heel, clamping onto his shoe, and Snake continued to walk with it across the basketball courts, limping slightly, his right foot clanking each time he brought it to the ground.

"What an idiot," Will said.

"You think he'll graduate?"

"In five years."

"I say six."

A plane roared in the sky, but I couldn't see it.

A breeze hit us and Will shivered.

Before I could figure out if he wanted to talk or not, he said, "She's ignoring my calls."

I scooted down so we were sitting on the same row. "What happened?"

"She didn't want to go to Christopher's thing. She wanted to be together, just the two of us, and talk about what we were going to do." Will paused and looked at the track houses on the other side of the soccer field. "I said I needed to get hammered, and she got pissed and said I didn't care about her. I told her that wasn't true and to calm down, but I really needed to cut loose and not think about it for one night. She said I shouldn't be thinking about anything else."

"I feel like it's sort of my fault," I admitted.

"Don't be stupid," he said. "I did it to myself. I mean, we did."

I turned to Will. "We did?"

"Me and Suji," he clarified.

Another breeze. This time I shivered.

"Then what happened?"

"I told her maybe we should take a break from each other and then she hung up on me."

The whole time he was talking, I pictured Suji and him arguing in a room or a parked car, somewhere private and face-to-face—*not* over the phone. I figured it out then that Will had probably instigated the fight, that he'd wanted to break up with Suji rather than deal with their situation.

"Now she won't return my messages," he continued.

"Did you try calling her today?"

"This morning I did. I got her voice mail again." Will's right leg began to bounce nervously. "She must hate my guts now."

Will obviously felt guilty for what he had done. He

117

was glum-faced and slouched as if gravity pulled on him harder than anyone else. I felt sorry for him, but at the same time I thought he was an asshole. What kind of guy gets a girl pregnant and then dumps her?

"I've got to go," I said, and stuck out my arm toward Will. We clasped hands. "Take it easy, man."

"Later," he said.

I left Will to his thoughts and pretended to hurry off to my next class. When I reached the gymnasium, I glanced back just as I was rounding the corner. Will was still sitting by himself on the bleachers, a stone caught between the bars of a sewer grate.

ISABEL

On Valentine's Day, between third and fourth period, I was walking with Vanessa down the hallway along with the herd of other students, the din of their small talk and gossip and insults. There was a large banner taped above the lockers that reminded everyone about the school dance that evening. The letters shimmered with glitter, hearts cut from pink construction paper glued to the corners. Two cherubs hovered on each side of the banner, their bows loaded with arrows. Vanessa pointed at the sign. "So are we going or what?"

"Did you go to school dances at Wilson?" I asked Vanessa.

"Yeah."

"Were they lame?"

"No, not really."

"Ours are really lame," I said.

A girl strained at her locker until it shuddered open. A boy dropped some papers and another boy laughed. Mr. Bissell, my geometry teacher from last year, walked past and someone said, "Look at that square!" Mr. Bissell whipped his head around and frowned at everyone.

"Come on, it'll be fun," Vanessa pleaded. "You, me, and Heidi."

"Heidi will *definitely* not want to go."

"If I can convince her, will you go?"

I turned to Vanessa. "There's no way Heidi will want to go. She hates dances more than I do."

"But what if I can convince her?"

I said nothing. A boy rushing down the hall twisted his body and threaded between Vanessa and me. "Samantha, wait!" he shouted.

I could feel Vanessa's eyes on me. "Well?"

"Okay," I said, caving. "But don't get your hopes up."

Right when we reached the corner where the hallways intersected, this boy collided into Vanessa and she nearly dropped her books. He quickly jerked his arms out and cradled them in case they tumbled. *"Whoa,"* he said. "You got 'em?"

"Yeah, yeah," Vanessa said.

"I'm sorry. I should've signaled."

Then I noticed the boy that this boy was walking with. It was Carlos, the museum guard.

"Isabel," he said, smiling.

"Hey," I said.

Vanessa straightened her books in her arms like a loose deck of cards. "Hi, Carlos." She gestured with her head at the boy who'd bumped into her. "This guy your friend?"

"Yep. This is Snake," he said.

Snake raised his hand up to his shoulder. "Yo," he said.

"Are you guys going to the dance tonight?" Carlos asked.

"I'm not sure," Vanessa said, looking in my direction.

"*Someone* told me they're lame."

"They're not if you have a few in the parking lot." Snake made a hang loose sign and put his thumb to his lips, then raised his pinkie toward the ceiling.

"Oh, you're a bad boy, aren't you?" Vanessa said coyly.

Snake grinned. "So I've been told," he said, leaning against the wall, his eyes leveled at her.

I turned to Carlos. "Thanks for the licorice the other day."

He smiled. "You're welcome."

"It's all this guy eats," Snake said. "It's like his pacifier or something."

Carlos socked Snake on the arm.

"It's true, dude."

"You guys want to know why we call Snake 'Snake'?" Carlos asked us.

"Sure," Vanessa said.

"In health ed. last semester—"

Snake grabbed on to Carlos and tried to cover his mouth. "Shut your piehole," he said.

Carlos wiggled free. *"Chill."*

"Aw, come on, let's hear it," Vanessa pleaded.

Snake shook his head sheepishly.

"When he's not around, I'll tell you," Carlos told Vanessa.

"Man, that's messed up," Snake said.

"I want to know too," I said, but what I really meant was, *I want you to talk to me too, Carlos.* I was surprised to find myself thinking like that about a guy.

"So you guys want to go to the dance or what?" he asked. Carlos turned to me, then Vanessa, then back to me.

"Sure, why not," I said. I turned to Vanessa and she had this oh-my-look-how-quickly-you've-changed-your-mind look on her face.

"Cool, we'll see you guys tonight then," Snake said, but he was just looking at Vanessa, his left hand flat against the wall, as if he were stopping it from falling down on us.

Soon as I got home from school I went to my room and played the latest Death Cab for Cutie CD for the hundredth time. I opened the closet and went through all my clothes, sliding the hangers across the bar one by one and pulling down outfits that I possibly might wear. Skirts, tops, jeans, sweaters, a couple dresses. I dumped them all on my bed and through a process of elimination I decided on a rose-colored dress and a black button-up sweater, both relatively new.

There was a knock at my door and I turned down the volume on my stereo.

"Come in," I said.

My mom opened the door. She was holding her coffee mug, the happy-face one with the pinwheeling eyes. "You're going somewhere?" she asked, blowing into her steaming cup.

"There's a dance at Millikan," I said.

"On a school night?"

"I won't be home late."

She took a sip and brought her mug down. "How late is not late?"

"Eleven?"

"Ten," she said sternly.

I clicked my tongue and frowned.

"Izzy, I thought you didn't like school dances."

I shoved my hands in my pockets and lifted my shoulders. "This guy asked me."

My mom's eyebrows went up. "Oh yeah? Who?"

"Just some guy. He works at the museum with Vanessa."

"I'm happy for you," she said. "I know how rough this past year has been."

"It has," I said.

There was a long pause, both of us thinking of Gabriel but neither of us wanting to say his name out loud.

"So, am I going to meet this guy tonight or what?" she asked.

I shook my head. "I'm driving with Vanessa. We're meeting up with him and his friend at the dance."

She leaned against the doorframe. "You know, when I was your age, the boys would always pick up the girls."

"Things have changed since the sixties," I told her.

My mom put her hand on her waist. "Excuse me?" she said in this high-pitched voice.

"What?"

"The *sixties*?"

I shrugged.

"Try the seventies, young lady," she said. "Nineteen seventy-eight, as a matter of fact."

"Oh," I said. "Sorry."

She blew into her cup. "You're lucky you're my daughter," she muttered.

"Why're you drinking coffee now?" I asked.

"It's green tea, actually. My stomach hasn't been feeling right." My mom placed her palm on her belly.

"Stomachache?"

"Yeah, I think so," she said. "I like that sweater."

I lifted the black sweater up from my bed and held it under my chin. "Me too," I said. I bit my lower lip. "How about ten-thirty?"

My mom took another sip of her tea.

"Please."

She brought her mug down. "Okay, but I want you *inside* the house at ten-thirty. If it's ten-thirty-one, you're grounded for a month."

"I won't be late," I said. "I promise."

My mom turned away from the doorframe and headed down the hallway. "The sixties," she said over her shoulder. "I should ground you anyway for *that*."

I closed my bedroom door. My cell rang and I looked at the digital display. It was Vanessa.

"Hey," I said. "I was just about to call you."

"Did you ask Heidi if she wanted to go?"

I was silent. After we had bumped into Carlos and Snake in the hallway, I told Vanessa that I'd call Heidi and ask if she wanted to join us. Truth is, I only wanted it to be us four. I figured Heidi would've just been an eye-rolling fifth wheel.

"You didn't ask her, did you?" Vanessa said.

"Nuh-uh."

"Is," she practically screamed into my ear.

"I'm telling you, Heidi *hates* school dances," I said. "She'd rather stay home and fantasize about guys than actually talk to one."

"Shouldn't you at least ask her? I mean, won't she be pissed if she found out that we went without her?"

I bit on my thumbnail. "She might."

"I don't want Heidi to hate me." Vanessa lowered her voice. "Sometimes I feel like she wishes it was just the two of you."

"That's not true," I said, although I got the same vibe. The way Heidi would slowly turn her back on Vanessa, how easily she'd dismiss one of her suggestions or ask a question while Vanessa was telling a story. Last week, when Vanessa was telling us about the day she fainted on a hiking trip, Heidi asked me, *Would you do Curtis Bradfield?* I scrunched up my forehead and shook my head no and turned my attention back to Vanessa, who had this perplexed look on her face. *Go on*, I'd told her, my hand on her arm.

"Well, I still think one of us should ask her," Vanessa said. "And by one of us, I mean you."

"The thing is, Vanessa, *they* asked *us*," I said. "Didn't they?"

She was quiet for a while, thinking. "Yeah, but still . . ."

"She won't find out," I said. "Even if she does, she'll be more mad at me than you."

"That's comforting."

I heard Roland in the backyard yell, "Gotcha!" I went to the window and peered through the curtains just as he was stepping out of the flower beds, his right fist in the air as if he were holding an imaginary sword.

"Besides, it'll be more fun with just the two of us," I said.

"You mean four," Vanessa added.

"There you go!"

Vanessa chuckled. I loved her laugh.

"I'll come pick you up at eight," I told her.

After I got off the phone I turned up the volume on my stereo and placed my outfit back inside the closet, on the far left of the rail. I sat on the ground and went through my pile of shoes, setting aside a pair of black heels. In my periphery I saw my bedroom door slowly crack open. "Mom," I said, more like a question. Roland's fist appeared just above the carpet and before I could figure out what was going on, a lizard as long as my forearm was inside my room. I screamed. Roland slammed the door. The lizard tilted its head, its beady black eyes looking right at me. I scooted away from the door, toward my dresser, the stereo booming over my head. Over the music, I could hear my brother giggling behind the door, and I thought, *I'm going to smack him.* The lizard scampered along the wall, its short, scaly legs high-stepping on the carpet as it slipped underneath my bed, hiding like a secret in the shadow of the mattress. And then I had another thought: *Heidi's going to find out.*

CARLOS

It had been exactly one week since Mira and I had split up, and I felt surprisingly good. There was no tightness in my throat when I thought about her, no wallowing or spasm in the heart. *It takes half the amount of time that you were with that person,* I kept thinking. But I felt healed already like a shaman had swatted my chest a couple times with palm leaves and chanted some indiscernible words. And this was before Snake opened the first thermos and poured me a plastic cupful of cranberry juice spiked with vodka. Actually, it was more like vodka spiked with cranberry juice.

I gulped from my cup and shuddered. It felt as though a hot wind crashed through me before whooshing off somewhere else. "Damn," I said. "That shit's *potent.*"

Snake tipped his cup back and swallowed. He wagged his head violently and made a sound with his lips loosened like a popped tire flapping around a car rim. *"Yowza,"* he said.

From where we stood in the school parking lot we could see the open double doors of the gymnasium, colors vibrating inside as if fireworks were exploding on the parquet floor. A one-two beat thumped within the high walls and I imagined the gym had a heart.

Snake craned his neck and surveyed the parking lot from one end to the other. "Man, where are the hoochie mamas?"

"They'll be here," I said. "Just chill."

"Why didn't you tell me about Vanessa before?"

I leaned against Snake's car. "Tell you what?"

"That you work with this hot chick at the museum."

I took a sip and wiped my mouth with the back of my

hand. "I didn't think she was your type."

"Hell yeah, she is," he said, like it was the most obvious thing in the world.

"How the hell am I supposed to know what's your type?"

"I know *yours*."

"Oh yeah? What's mine?" I asked.

Snake grinned. "Male."

I finished my cup and held it toward Snake for a refill. "I can't wait to tell Vanessa how you got your nickname."

Snake unscrewed the thermos and poured me another drink. "Go for it, I don't care." He topped off his cup before screwing the cap back on, then set the thermos inside his car through the open window on the driver's side. "Just leave out the part about me pissing on myself."

"Are you kidding me?" I said. "That's the best part."

Headlights lit up the pavement behind Snake's car and we hid our cups behind our legs. A black Pontiac slowly rolled our way, balls of light from the lampposts glided over the curved hood like a school of electrical fish. The driver was a brown-skinned boy with a shaved head, his elbow jutting out the window. He stopped the car right behind Snake's and waved us over with two fingers.

"What does he want?" Snake asked.

"How should I know," I said.

The boy revved his engine and stared us down. Shadows filled his eye sockets and made it look as if he were wearing sunglasses.

I put my cup down. "Screw it," I said, and walked over to the car.

The boy had sleepy eyes and a patch of hair the size of a postage stamp below his bottom lip. Once I crouched down I noticed the girl smoking in the passenger seat, her hair black and straight. The end of her cigarette glowed inside the car's dark interior like a red firefly, hovering from her mouth to her lap and back to her mouth. What I had mistaken for a mole on the corner of the boy's eye was actually a green tattoo of a teardrop. Another tattoo coiled up his neck from under his white T, the word *Angel* in a script font that reminded me of Richard Spurgeon's neon sign. "Got any weed?" the boy finally said.

"Nah, man," I replied.

"You want some?"

"I'm all right."

He flicked his head toward Snake. "What about your homie?"

The girl clicked her tongue. It sounded like the rasp of the wheel on a lighter. "Let's go, Rico," she said, irritated.

He quickly turned to her, his jaw muscle twitching. "What did I tell you?" he said. There was another tattoo that ran down the nape of his neck, another word, this one in Old English script. I could only make out the first two letters: *CL*. The rest were tucked underneath his shirt, and I wondered what the word might be. *CLOAK, CLOUD, CLOCK, CLAMOR...*

The girl took a drag from her cigarette and the tip burned brighter.

Rico turned back to me, his face rigid. "Go ask your homie."

I stood up and walked back to Snake, casually, even though my legs wanted to run.

"He wants to know if you want any weed," I said when I was standing beside him.

Snake shook his head. "Nuh-uh."

"You need to tell him."

"Why?"

"Just tell him," I hissed.

Snake lifted his hand and leaned to one side like a student in the back row with a question. *"No weed for me,"* he hollered.

I dropped my face into my palm. The car skidded off behind me, the engine roared down the parking lot. We watched the black Pontiac pull into traffic and fly down the street. A car horn blared in the distance.

"That was dumb of me," Snake said.

"No shit."

"I wasn't thinking."

"He's in a gang, too."

"For real?"

I picked up my cup from where I had left it and took a big swallow. I imagined the boy coming back in another car, one filled with other boys. I imagined the silver eye of a gun barrel staring from the backseat.

The gymnasium's heart kept beating across the parking

lot, the inside blushing crimson, blue, lime, the outlines of students pulsing the same colors. I looked at Snake. He was biting the inside of his cheek, working the soft flesh.

"Don't worry about it," I said.

Snake took another gulp and smacked his lips, exhaling loudly. "I think I put in too much vodka," he said, steering the conversation from one incompetent act to another.

"Yes, you did." I held my cup by the rim with my fingertips and swirled my drink around.

"I'm not a bartender," he said.

"Maybe you should go to bartending school," I told him.

"Dude, there's no such thing as bartending school."

"You want to bet?"

Snake lowered his cup. "You're shitting me."

"You know Jonathan Meeks?"

"That tall dude?"

I nodded. "His brother's in bartending school."

"Man, I should do *that*. Bartenders are always getting laid." Snake took a swig and looked into his cup as if there were a goldfish swimming in it. "Soon as I get out of this shithole, that's what I'm doing."

Again the ground behind Snake's car lit up with headlights. We moved our cups behind our legs once more and tried to look normal, not like two teenagers getting hammered in the parking lot.

A car horn chirped, and we both turned around quickly. It was Isabel, wavy-haired and green-eyed Isabel.

Vanessa leaned out from the passenger seat and shouted, "What're you guys doing?"

Snake and I lifted our cups as if we were making a toast.

Isabel smiled and shook her head slowly. "We'll be back." She hit the gas and rolled off to find parking, sparks of light sliding along the car's frame.

"She's hella cute," I told Snake.

"So's Vanessa."

"I think she digs me."

"Vanessa?"

"No, dipshit. Isabel."

"Yeah, I think she does," Snake said. "But Vanessa's

got a better booty." He palmed an imaginary ass in front of him and moved his hips suggestively.

I finished my drink and watched Isabel's car glide down the parking lot and turn around. "There was something between us when we met," I said.

"Between you and Vanessa?"

I flicked Snake on the side of his head and my finger thumped against his skull. *"Isabel,"* I corrected him.

"Shit, man, I thought you were talking about Vanessa again," Snake said. "I know you work both at the museum with you."

"What?" I said, laughing. "Did you hear what you just said?"

Snake blinked.

"You said, *You work both at the museum with you.*"

"I did?"

Even though we were standing just outside a lamp-post's circle of light, there was enough illumination for me to see that Snake's eyes were now glassy.

"Are you drunk already?" I asked him.

"I'm cool," he said.

"Sure you are," I said. "You lightweight."

"Bitch, what are you talking about? I can drink more than you." Then, as if to prove his point, Snake lifted his cup to his lips and tipped his head back, finishing his drink in one quick motion. "Just like water," he said.

Isabel and Vanessa walked toward us through the parking lot, chatting quietly. Isabel wore a dark red dress with a black sweater. Her hair drifted behind her.

"Hey, guys," Vanessa said.

"Hello, ladies," Snake said. "Would any of you care for a drink?"

"You look nice," I told Isabel.

"Thanks," she said. "You too." She crossed her arms, then uncrossed them. She did this thing with her mouth, a quick smile that pushed her cheeks out like a chipmunk's.

"What're you guys drinking?" Vanessa asked.

Snake reached through the driver's-side window and pulled out the thermos and a plastic cup. "Cranberry and vodka."

"Isn't that a Sea-Breeze?" Vanessa asked.

"More like a Sea-Hurricane," I said.

Snake handed Vanessa the cup and she raised it to her nose and whiffed. She took a sip and made a sour face. "Oh *God*," she said. "How could you *drink* that?"

"Easy," Snake bragged.

"Do you have anything else?"

"I've got another thermos with OJ and vodka."

A car rolled toward us and we hid our cups. It was Mr. Ziolkowski, folded inside his Jetta. He was hunched over the steering wheel, his forehead inches from the windshield. He gazed in our direction and waved.

"We should probably drink in your car," I told Snake. "Play it safe."

"Good idea," Isabel said.

Snake climbed behind the wheel and leaned over to open the passenger-side door for Vanessa. I let Isabel into the backseat first before I scooted next to her. She smelled like vanilla and flowers, her hair or skin, I couldn't tell which.

Snake put his key into the ignition and turned it halfway so the console lit up blue. A song filled the car with a thick bass and lazy drumbeat, a woman's voice threading through the rhythm. Snake eased the volume down and uncapped the thermos. "Screwdriver, anyone?" he asked.

Vanessa held her cup out and Snake filled it. She brought her drink to her lips tentatively and sipped. "Much better," she said.

Snake filled another cup and passed it to Isabel. "There you go," he said. "Drink that so Carlos has a chance."

Isabel did that chipmunk smile again—a nervous twitch, my guess.

I reached over the seat and thumped Snake on the skull as hard as I could.

"Ow!" he exclaimed. *"Man."*

"You deserved that," Vanessa said.

Snake looked at her. "Babe, that hurts."

Vanessa cocked her head to one side and raised her eyebrows. "Babe? You're already calling me babe?" She jabbed her finger at Snake's waist.

"Don't," he said, dropping his elbow and backing off. "I'm ticklish."

She poked him again.

"So you guys want to know how Snake got his nick-name or what?" I asked.

"Yes," Isabel and Vanessa said in unison, excited.

"Don't tell them the part I told you not to tell," Snake reminded me.

"You mean when you pissed in your pants? That part?" I said.

Vanessa nearly choked on her drink.

"Oh, this is going to be *good*," Isabel said.

"Screw it. Tell 'em everything." Snake waved his hand around like a magician after performing a trick.

"This happened last year, in Ms. Wagner's health class," I began. "Me and Snake sat next to each other in the back."

"What's your real name, by the way?" Vanessa asked.

"Jeffrey," Snake said.

I reached over with my cup and motioned for Snake to fill it. "So anyway, Ms. Wagner was showing us this video on snakebites, about what steps to take if you're ever bitten by a poisonous snake. The dramatizations were so lame."

Snake unscrewed the thermos. "They were *really* lame.

Remember the park ranger with the knee-high socks?"

"Don't interrupt," Vanessa said, poking. "Go on, Carlos."

"It was pretty hysterical. I mean, they had this guy hobbling back to his campsite, wincing. Then he showed his friend his leg and the snakebite looked so phony, like someone made two dots with a red felt pen." I took a sip from my cup. "Me and Snake were laughing, everyone's laughing, and Ms. Wagner was getting mad, shushing us. Then the video switched to these color photographs of untreated snakebites."

"It was gnarly," Snake said.

"They showed these hands that were all swollen and black. The fingers looked like burnt sausages."

Vanessa twisted up her face. *"Gross."*

"One of the photos was of this dude's leg, his calf," I continued. "It was fat and purple and all shiny like an eggplant. Then they showed the same leg split open during surgery and we got to see what the poison had done to the muscle. Really nasty stuff."

"It sounds like it," Isabel said.

I took another sip. "In the corner of my eye I see Snake lean my way, like he wants to whisper something to me. Next thing I know—*Wham!*—he's on the floor."

Isabel covered her mouth. "Oh my God."

"You fainted?" Vanessa asked.

"Yeah," Snake said shyly.

"Hey, I fainted on a hike once."

"All right." Snake made a fist and held it in front of Vanessa. "Fist bump," he said.

Vanessa tapped Snake's fist softly with her own and giggled.

"Anyway, someone hit the lights and there was Snake sprawled out on the floor. All of a sudden, there was a wet spot on the crotch of his jeans, getting bigger and bigger."

"Aw, poor baby wet his diaper," Vanessa teased.

Snake nodded sheepishly.

"Ms. Wagner kneeled at his side and all the students crowded around. Eventually Snake came to, like he was waking from a big nap."

"I was so damn confused," Snake said. "I didn't know

how the hell I ended up on the floor."

"Then what happened?" Vanessa asked, sipping her drink.

"He sat back down on his chair and started to rub his noggin, like this." I demonstrated, sliding my palm across my forehead. "Then Ms. Wagner asked me to walk him to the school nurse."

"Poor you," Vanessa said, caressing Snake's arm. She turned to me. "Weren't you scared when it happened?"

"Yeah," I said. "But when he woke up, then it was funny as shit."

"What a friend," Snake said.

Vanessa rubbed Snake's arm again. "Are you wearing Huggies now?"

Everyone laughed but Isabel. She was looking out the car window, across the parking lot, her eyes frozen on some faraway object. I tried to figure out what it was that held her attention, but there was nothing out there but a row of houses sunk in darkness and a lone streetlamp's yellow halo.

"Wow, that's a great story," Vanessa said. She turned

around in her seat. "Right, Isabel?"

She kept staring out the window.

"Is," Vanessa said.

Still nothing.

"Is!" Vanessa shouted.

ISABEL

I snapped out of my tunnel vision, my daydreaming, whatever you want to call it, and looked at Vanessa and Snake and Carlos, all of whom were looking at me.

"Sorry," I said. "I was just thinking."

"Obviously," Vanessa said.

Carlos put his hand gently on my leg. "Is everything okay?"

"Yeah, I'm fine," I said. "I zone out sometimes, that's all." I took a big gulp from my drink and smiled.

It was happening more and more frequently—spacing

out. Anything could set me off. A struck match, a car horn, windblown trees, a stranger's cough. This time it was the image of Snake tipping over, the whack of his body as he hit the classroom floor. I started wondering what it would feel like to faint, what happens to the brain, if it's anything like death or if it's more like sleeping, a quick nap. And then I wondered what happens the instant you die—the exact moment—if it's like a light switch turned off and the room is suddenly dark, or was it the opposite, a million lights blazing. But wouldn't someone need their eyes to see that being dead was complete darkness or complete brightness, and wouldn't that be impossible, the person being dead and all, including the eyes, and is that why humans came up with the idea of the soul and heaven and religion, because an afterlife that consisted of nothing but nothing was too hard to visualize, too lonely to imagine?

This got me thinking of Gabriel, of the photos I took of him with my digital camera and clicked through on my computer the other day. Gabriel on the bleachers, Gabriel striking a pose in a sombrero, Gabriel in the swimming pool with the water up to his neck, hair slicked back, the shadow of a palm tree behind him on a wall like a twelve-fingered hand reaching. A wave of guilt slammed into me and I began to kick myself for thinking I was ready to be with another guy. Maybe I needed a couple more weeks. A few more months. Another year. Maybe my heart would never be ready.

"Is!" Vanessa shouted again, breaking my spell.

Carlos removed his hand from my leg, Vanessa turned back around in her seat, and Snake unscrewed the thermos and filled his cup once more.

"Shit, Carlos, I forgot to tell you," Snake said. "Will wanted you to call him."

Carlos leaned forward. "Did he say what it was about?"

"He didn't. Probably Suji."

"Suji Kim?" I asked.

"You know her?"

"She's in my English class," I said. "She hasn't been there for the past two days, though."

Carlos leaned back in his seat and made a sound in his throat, a short hum. "When did you talk to him?"

"Just before I left to pick you up," Snake said.

Carlos took out his cell phone and checked his messages. "This is probably him," he said, and lowered his head, listening.

"You good back there?" Snake said. He shook the thermos and the booze sloshed inside of it.

"Yeah, I'm good," I said, then took a sip from my cup. I heard some kids laughing in the parking lot behind me, the chime of a kicked bottle skittering across the blacktop. I looked over my shoulder and saw them heading toward the gymnasium, one boy already dancing, his hands pushing upward as if he were lifting a heavy box.

"You want to go inside?" Carlos asked me, slipping his phone back into his front pocket.

"Sure," I said, even though I wasn't sure. The guilt was still swirling around me.

"I should warn you, Is," Snake said. "Carlos looks like he's being stung by bees when he dances."

"Dude, you should talk." Carlos turned to me. "You know those dolls you see on dashboards with the springy necks?"

"You mean a bobble head?"

151

"Yeah, those things. Snake dances like a bobble head in a car going over potholes."

Vanessa was in mid-sip and quickly covered her mouth to stop from spraying orange juice and vodka all over the windshield. Her shoulders quaked, she held her laughter inside her mouth with her drink. Finally she composed herself and gulped it all down. She laughed and coughed, fanning her face with her hand. *"Almost,"* she said, giggling. "That was *close.*"

"I laughed Pepsi out of my nose once when I was a kid," Snake said.

"God, you're really turning me on," Vanessa said, still chuckling. "Pepsi out of your nose, piss in your jeans. You're a *keeper.*"

Then we were all laughing. Even Snake.

"Let's go inside and tear up the dance floor," Carlos said, already opening the door.

Snake whispered something to Vanessa, and Vanessa whispered something back. I finished my drink and set it down on the floor of the car.

"We'll meet you guys inside," Snake said.

Carlos and I looked at each other. There was a pause there, a moment when we both weighed the idea of spending a few minutes alone. "Come on," he said.

I put my hand on Vanessa's shoulder. "Don't be long."

Vanessa covered my hand with hers and turned her head so I saw her profile in the console's glow, the powder blue line from forehead to chin. "We won't be," she said.

I stepped out into the cool evening and straightened my sweater. The gymnasium was at the end of the parking lot and I could see kids inside the front entrance, their silhouettes, the wall flashing orange and yellow like they were standing around a bonfire.

Carlos blew into his cupped hands. "Chilly."

"I've got my sweater," I said, stating the obvious.

"It's nice."

"Thanks."

"I like the buttons."

I held one of the pearly white beads and rolled it between my thumb and forefinger. "Me too," I said.

We began walking across the parking lot. Whenever we decided to zigzag between cars, Carlos let me go first. I thought it was really sweet, but then I thought maybe he wanted to check out my ass.

"Sorry about Snake," he said.

"What do you mean?"

"That comment he made about drinking so I'd have a chance."

"Oh," I said. "I thought that was kind of funny."

"He likes to embarrass me. If we're in an elevator with other people, or in a line for a movie, he'll say really loud, *So, how's your rash doing?* or something like that."

"I'd be afraid to go out with him in public," I said.

"I guess I'm sort of used to it."

We had to zigzag through a couple more cars and Carlos slowed down. "After you," he said.

I smiled and walked ahead of him, hoping my sweater and dress didn't make my ass look too big.

We stepped onto the walkway that cut through the grass and straight to the gymnasium's front doors. The speakers thumped louder as we approached, the lights flashed brighter, white and pink now. I heard the chatter and laughter of students inside, their voices coming in and out of the music's crashing waves.

Mr. Bissell and Ms. Lauden were seated behind a table just outside the entrance. There was a fat red roll of raffle tickets and a clipboard with a pencil tied to the metal clasp. Mr. Bissell picked up the pencil and made two quick lines on a sheet that was already crowded with marks.

"Here you go," Ms. Lauden chimed, tearing off a couple raffle tickets and handing them to us. "We're giving away a gift bag at the end of the dance."

"What's in the gift bag?" Carlos asked.

"It's a *surprise*."

Mr. Bissell muttered something under his breath and Ms. Lauden elbowed him playfully.

When we stepped into the gymnasium we were slammed with the music and splashed with colored lights. The air was warm from the heat of other bodies as we shuffled past one of the throbbing speakers, my dress vibrating against my skin. The DJ stood on a platform with headphones and bobbed his head like a parrot. Carlos took my hand and together we maneuvered through the flailing crowd, the maze of dancing bodies. Once he found a good spot, he turned around and said something that sounded like, *Take chances like this.*

"*What?*" I yelled.

"*Snake dances like this,*" Carlos shouted, then he jerked his head forward and back, forward and back, his mouth slightly open. Good thing I wasn't drinking then or else I would've showered Carlos with orange juice and vodka.

"*Oh my God, that's hilarious.*"

"*What?*"

I bracketed my mouth with my hands. *You're hilarious.*"

Carlos smiled and then we started dancing for real. A disco ball twirled somewhere and pieces of light swam across our faces. Hearts were taped haphazardly along the gymnasium wall, twinkling with glitter. A girl bumped into me from behind and shouted, "*Sorry!*"

When a red balloon bounced our way, I slapped at it and it bounced off Carlos's head. I covered my mouth with both hands.

"*You did that on purpose!*" he hollered.

"I swear I didn't!"

"I'll remember that!"

"It's hot in here!"

"What?!"

I leaned in close to him, right by his neck. *"I said it's hot in here!"*

"You want to step out for a while?"

I nodded and he took my hand again, my sweaty hand, and we slipped out of the crowd toward the gymnasium's back entrance. When Carlos opened the double doors, a heart that was cut from construction paper and folded in half fell like a heavy leaf at our feet. "Whoa, whoa," a boy said, jamming his shoe in between the doors before it closed. He picked up the folded heart and placed it over the lock, then carefully closed the door so the heart poked out like an arrowtip.

"Sorry about that," Carlos said.

"No worries," the boy said. His pupils were dilated, his dark hair curly and big as a pom-pom. He ambled over to his friends leaning against a chain-link fence where a girl dipped her face into a jacketed boy's lifted palm. She snorted loudly and tossed her head back as if a car had rear-ended her. She pinched her nose, rubbed it, then pinched it again.

I must've had a strange look on my face because Carlos asked me, "Want to go back inside?"

"Yeah," I said. "Vanessa and Snake are probably looking for us."

"They're probably still in the car."

"You think?"

Carlos grabbed the folded heart and opened the door and slipped it back over the latch once we were inside. The DJ was now playing a ballad. Blue lights turned the gymnasium into a giant aquarium where kids slow-danced in the water, their indigo faces shiny with sweat. I saw a couple kiss in the sway of bodies and I thought of Gabriel, his face and how he died, his eyes and how he laughed, barely making a sound, like he was laughing behind thick glass. Maybe it was the booze, maybe because Carlos was holding my hand, but at that moment I didn't feel sad at all, or guilty for *not* feeling sad. I scanned the room, the blue bodies turning slowly, looking for Vanessa and Snake.

"I don't see them," I told Carlos.

"Snake doesn't slow-dance," he said.

"Do you?" I asked him, but he didn't hear me. Or he did and pretended that he didn't.

Carlos led me to the front entrance and once again we were outside, standing before Mr. Bissell and Ms. Lauden. The pencil marks on the clipboard looked the same as when we'd entered.

"That was quick," Ms. Lauden said.

"We're actually looking for our friends," Carlos said. "Snake—I mean Jeffrey McKenzie."

"And Vanessa Barcelos," I added.

"Jeffrey is one of my students," Mr. Bissell said. "First period."

"Did he come inside after we did?"

"No, he didn't," he said.

Ms. Lauden shrugged.

We turned away from the table and headed back to the car, following our footsteps, zigzagging the same way across the parking lot that we had come. A siren wailed in the distance.

"What if they're, you know . . ." Carlos said. He cleared his throat.

"I don't think they are," I said.

"Well, I know how Snake is."

"I know how Vanessa is, and she wouldn't do that with a guy she barely knows."

"How long have you known Vanessa?"

"That doesn't matter," I snapped.

Carlos chuckled. He had this I-know-all-the-answers look on his face.

I folded my arms, annoyed. Everything had been going so well up until that point.

"We'll see who's right," he said.

But there was nothing to see. Where Snake's car should've been there was now an empty parking spot. Just two parallel lines painted on the ground, an empty red cup on its side like the ones we were drinking from. A

160

breeze pushed the cup and it rolled back and forth along the same arc. We looked around the parking lot as if they had just pulled away, as if we could chase them down and stop them from going to wherever they were going.

CARLOS

By third period the next day, news of the accident was falling down all over Millikan like ash. Bits and pieces of information swirled to our ears. Some fit with each other, some didn't. According to one story, Snake ran a red light and sideswiped another car, killing himself and Vanessa. Another rumor had it that they'd both survived, but everyone in the car he hit, a family of four, was dead. I also heard he crashed into a utility pole, that nothing happened to Vanessa, just a few scratches here and there, but Snake was gone, crushed between his seat and steering wheel. I called Snake's cell repeatedly, but all I got was his voice mail: *Yo, leave me a message, beotch.*

I walked around campus, stunned, full of dread, my heart a chunk of ice inside my chest. Lockers slid by me, the gills of their vents, then the classroom doors, their taped flyers. I glided with the students in a daze, outside and across the quad with the screeching seagulls, the orange tables and green trees, the radiant blue California sky. Someone called my name and I turned around and there was Christopher Olsson, his worried eyes, asking me what I knew, telling me what he had heard, that Snake was hit by a drunk driver and was now dead. "Shit, man," he said, "last weekend he was at my party, laughing at my stoned dog, and now he's gone." I heard my name again and it was Mira, her eyes wet, one hand over her mouth. "What happened? I keep hearing different stories," she said. "Was he drinking? Were you with him last night at the dance? As soon as I heard, I thought of you. I'm sorry, Carlos, I'm so sorry. I'm here for you if you want to talk." I wondered what was true, what wasn't—dead or still breathing, both or just one, and if just one, who? Then Will's voice, Will's slackened face and hooded eyes, his shoulders hunched with the news.

"I just called his cell phone and his dad answered," he said. "He's at Long Beach Memorial."

I stood there and said nothing.

"His dad said he's on life support."

I listened.

"He asked if I gave him alcohol."

I stood there.

"He said if it wasn't me, then who ruined his child's life."

A seagull wheeled above us and squawked angrily, over and over, like nails yanked out of a piece of wood.

"I was hanging out with him last night," I finally said. "He was drinking. We both were."

"Let's go to the hospital," Will said. "I'll drive." We walked across the quad, past the administration building and into the school parking lot. The sun blazed above the gymnasium and every windshield flashed under its harsh light. Our shadows slid in front of us, our legs scissored the pavement—open, close, open, close. Someone shouted behind us, "Hey, where do you two think you're going?" It was an adult's voice, a teacher, maybe the principal, some authority who saw us as nothing more than delinquents skipping school. We ignored whoever it was and folded our bodies into Will's car and drove off.

The windows were rolled down and the air rushed over my arm, my shirtsleeve fluttering. We hit a red light on Willow and watched an old couple stroll arm-in-arm, their steps slow and measured, as if the crosswalk were a rickety bridge suspended over a canyon. On the freeway, as we were driving past the airport, I watched a 747 coming in for a landing, the wings and fuselage dazzling in the sunlight. Then Will pulled off the freeway and we headed south on Atlantic until we saw the L-shaped hospital looming to our right.

The glass doors at the hospital entrance opened automatically like the ones at the museum, and there, in the middle of the polished floors, underneath a skylight, was a circular planter made of concrete, a tree with a slim trunk and slimmer branches, shiny green leaves that looked almost plastic. Blue sofa chairs lined one wall where a man sat alone reading the newspaper, his torso and face hidden behind the newsprint. He coughed loudly and the paper shook in his hands and I wondered if Snake and Vanessa's story was already printed, their names quivering with the other words, or if their story was too new for ink.

I was sliding my finger down the hospital directory, trying to locate the Trauma Center, when Will whistled me over. He was already standing by the elevator, pushing the button repeatedly with his thumb. "I know where to go," he said.

Once we were both in the elevator, Will rested his head against the cold steel wall and stared up at the acrylic panels that shined from the tube lights above them. We swayed and moved upward, a low chime for every floor we passed, like a drop of water hitting a bell. I felt my stomach turn, anxiety pressing on my chest. I closed my eyes and pretended I was somewhere else, a hotel in Las Vegas, so that when the elevator doors finally opened I would be greeted by the noise and lights of a casino, plush red carpets and the clamor of a hundred slot machines, mirrors and laughter and the green velvet of poker tables, and rising up from all the chaos would be the siren of a jackpot, shrilling like a car alarm going off.

The elevator doors opened on a quiet waiting room, maroon sofa chairs lined up against two walls, more than half filled with visitors. A potted plant in the corner dangled its knife-shaped leaves beside a coffee table fanned with magazines.

I sat down beside an old man who smelled like mint aftershave, his knobby hands resting on his lap. Will went to the reception desk and talked to a woman in a baby yellow shirt with a name tag pinned over her heart. He leaned against the counter and said something to her. She tilted her head and said something back, then lifted the handset and spoke to someone on the other line. Will looked back my way and raised his hand with his palm up as if to say, *She doesn't know anything* or *We're not allowed to see Snake.* The woman hung up and said something to Will and he looked at his watch before walking back to the waiting room and sitting across from me. "Only family members are allowed to see him," he said.

"Shit," I said. "What should we do?"

Will stretched out his legs and positioned the heel of one shoe against the tip of the other. "I don't know, you tell me."

"Did you ask her how he was doing?"

"She said she didn't know."

"What about Vanessa?"

"I didn't ask," he said.

I went to the reception desk and waited for the woman to put down the receiver. Her name tag read ANDREA and she had a gold cross on her necklace. "Dr. Holman wants to run a couple more tests. . . ." she said to whoever she was talking to. "Yes, I understand. . . . Have a good afternoon." When she hung up, she scribbled something on a bright orange Post-it and attached it to the bottom of her monitor. She turned in her swivel chair to face me. "Yes?" she said.

"I was wondering if you know anything about Vanessa," I said. "She came in last night."

"What's her last name?"

I bit my bottom lip. "I don't remember," I said. "It begins with a B."

The receptionist fiddled with her gold cross, waiting for me to give her more information.

"She was in a car accident with my friend Jeffrey McKenzie."

"Is she a friend of yours also?"

"Yes. I work with her."

"What's your name?"

"Carlos," I said. "Carlos Delgado."

The woman let go of her cross and picked up the receiver. "I'll see what I can find out," she said.

I went back to my chair and slumped down into it and let my legs bounce nervously up and down.

"What did she say?" Will asked.

"Not much."

"Is she okay?"

"She didn't tell me anything," I said. "I know she knows something."

"Stupid bitch," Will muttered.

I looked around the waiting room.

A girl with a ponytail and ball cap talked softly into her cell phone, her hand cupping her words.

A man in a crisp white shirt and tie dug his finger into his ear and yawned.

A large woman in a flower-printed muumuu fidgeted with a Kleenex, twirling and pulling one end between her finger and thumb.

"Let me see your cell phone," I told Will.

He fished it out of his pocket and lobbed it to me, but when I flipped it open and looked at the keypad, I realized I didn't have Isabel's number.

The elevators dinged open and a black woman walked into the lobby with her two boys—twins, it appeared. They both wore the same jeans and green-striped shirt, the same little brown shoes. The woman shuffled to the reception desk while her boys followed behind, heads lowered, grief-stricken, one clutching a portable PlayStation, the other empty-handed. Their mother exchanged a few words with the receptionist before sitting down on a sofa chair near the coffee table. She picked up a *Newsweek* and flipped through the pages casually, her face a brown stone smoothed by water. Then her boys began jostling over the PlayStation. "It's my turn." "No it's not." "Give it to me."

"Stop it, Leo." "You've been hogging it all day." "No I haven't." Finally their mother slapped the magazine down on her lap and hissed at them.

Will stared at his watch as if he could make it go faster. Above his head was a painting of a boy in red swim trunks, shin-deep in water. He was setting down a toy sailboat and the water was full of ripples, the blue sky and the boy reflected in it—the red squiggles of his trunks, the beige and peach of his skin, the white sail like a cloth napkin dropped on the floor. I imagined a strong gust pushing the sailboat away from the boy and gliding out into the heart of the lake, getting smaller and smaller and smaller. . . .

"Are you Carlos?"

He wore a white coat, blue shirt and black tie, slacks and Nikes.

"Yeah," I said.

"I was told that you were inquiring about Ms. Barcelos."

"You mean Vanessa?" I asked, just to be sure.

"Yes." He took off his gold-rimmed specs. "Vanessa's

parents were here last night." He folded his glasses and slipped them into his coat pocket. "She didn't make it. We tried everything that we could, but her injuries were too severe and extensive."

The air was sucked out of me.

"Okay," I said.

He placed his hand on my shoulder briefly and gave it a little squeeze.

"Okay," I said again even though he hadn't said anything more.

"I'm sorry," he said.

I nodded and he walked away.

Will had his head lowered and his elbows resting on his knees, his hands clasped together. He looked up and met my eyes and then let his gaze slide off to the floor. He opened his mouth, but no words came out.

I felt my body getting heavier, or rather I felt the world around me getting lighter. It was as if I were on an elevator, dropping floor by floor, while everything around me stayed where it was. The walls. The maroon chairs. The receptionist. The painting. Will. The ponytailed girl. The yawning man. The black woman. Her sulking twins. The large woman. Her dress crowded with flowers. The tissue she twirled and twirled into a candlewick.

ISABEL

It was almost a year to the day when Gabriel's car went into the canal, and I couldn't help but think Vanessa's death and his were somehow related. It felt like some sick joke, a cosmic prank that's only played on an unlucky few. I barricaded myself in my room, swaddled myself in bed-covers, and cried for hours. For both of them.

Late in the afternoon, when I looked at my reflection in the bathroom mirror, my eyes were all puffy and red, my skin was pale, more like dough than flesh. My dark hair, which was normally wavy, now hung limply to my shoulders. I didn't bother to swipe any lipstick across my lips, so my mouth looked chapped and bloodless. Grief had turned my face into a stranger's. It was if I were looking at a sister I never knew I had, an older sister who lived in another state, who'd gone through many hardships and now was coming home, looking for shelter.

The doorbell rang and I went to answer it, brushing my hair with my fingertips. Heidi stood on the front porch with the same look of despair. The whites of her eyes were pink, her shoulders hunched. Above my neighbor's house across the street, dusk had turned the sky into different shades of maroon and orange like the skin of a nectarine.

Heidi sniffled. "You ready?"

"Let me get a sweatshirt," I said.

In my bedroom, my mom came in and gave me a hug from behind. She kissed the top of my head. "We can talk some more when you get back," she said.

I pulled my mint green sweatshirt from the hanger and slipped it on. My mom lifted my hair over the hood and smoothed it down with her hands. "Maybe you should wear your jacket instead. You might get cold."

"I'll be fine."

"Please don't come home too late."

I grabbed the plastic bag on my bed with the two vanilla candles inside. "I won't."

"When's the funeral?" she asked.

"Sunday."

"I could go with you if you'd like."

"You don't have to," I said.

She brushed her hand down my hair again. "After school tomorrow, we can find a nice dress."

"Okay."

She kissed the top of my head again. "I love you, Izzy."

"I love you too," I said.

When I stepped outside, Heidi was sitting on the curb next to her car, buckled over and sobbing. I sat down on the curb and wrapped my arms around her.

"I wasn't nice to her," she said. "I didn't want her to get too close to you."

"It's okay, Heidi," I said, rubbing her back.

"I was jealous. I'd see how you two were with each

other and I'd start hating her." Heidi wiped her eyes with the cuff of her sweater. "I wanted it like it was, just the two of us. And now it is."

"Don't do this to yourself," I told her.

"I got what I wanted."

"Don't, Heidi."

"I'm not a good person."

"Yes, you are," I said. I brushed her hair away from her face.

"I'm sorry, Vanessa," she said.

Then we both cried on each other, right there on the curb in front of my house, the sky above us getting darker and darker, porch lights flickering on up and down the street.

We stopped by a flower shop on Spring Street and picked out a dozen yellow roses that were inside a tin vase. When we placed them on the counter, the store owner asked if we wanted any baby's breath. I shook my head no. "Just the roses," I said. The woman rang us up and I noticed that one of her hands was severely scarred as if by a fire, the skin stretched and marbled white and pink. Her other hand, smooth and beige, pressed the keys on the register. We left and the door chimed twice behind us.

We climbed back in the car and placed the roses in the backseat with the candles. We drove in silence, just the sound of the tires on the road and the quiet purr of the engine. I fiddled with the zipper on my sweatshirt, dragging the flat metal under my thumbnail as if I had some dirt there.

"I don't understand why they left us," I finally said.

Heidi looked at me and then back at the road. She rolled down her window, thin strands of her hair dancing around her face.

"They said they'd meet us inside the gym," I said. "They said they wouldn't be long."

"Where do you think they were heading?" Heidi asked.

"I have no idea."

We stopped at a traffic light. A car honked and another lurched forward. A motel's neon VACANCY sign blazed hot pink beside a palm tree. In the evening sky, the moon was almost full—a white balloon tethered to the roof of a liquor store.

"Maybe they were heading to his house," Heidi said.

"I don't think so."

"She was drinking, right?"

"We all were," I said, "but Vanessa and I only had one cup."

"I can't believe she's not here anymore."

More silence, more low hums from the engine.

"Neither can I," I said.

I watched the cars at the intersection turning left onto Los Coyotes. I watched the shadowy faces of every driver and wondered about their lives, if they were married or not, if they had kids, if someone they loved had passed away, if they were listening to music, if they were happy, if they were heading home, if they were lost.

The light turned green and we continued on down Spring, making a left and then a right and soon we were there. Heidi parked on a residential street lined with giant trees and I reached over into the backseat and grabbed the yellow roses, the bag of candles. I sat in the front seat for a while and closed my eyes, the flowers and candles on my lap, and breathed in the vanilla and roses.

When I stepped out of the car, Heidi was already on the sidewalk, gazing up at a second-story window. A light was on, and someone's shadow passed across the wall and folded at the ceiling like a paper doll in a book.

The trees loomed above us and swayed in the night wind, the leaves rustling faintly.

I joined Heidi on the sidewalk and together we walked to where it had happened, where a fire hydrant was sheared off and a wall smashed in, covered with a blue tarp. There were bricks and pieces of brick strewn on the sidewalk. It was as though we were standing at the foot of ancient ruins. Nearby was a framed photograph of Vanessa propped against the trunk of an oak. The photo was surrounded with roses and daisies and carnations, handwritten notes and cards. A brown teddy bear held on to a stuffed heart with *I Love You* embroidered into the fabric. On the curb, blown-out candles stood upright in their hardened puddles of wax.

Heidi covered her mouth and cried. I was all cried

out. I was an empty well, a vessel holding nothing but air and dust.

I walked over to Vanessa's photograph and placed the yellow roses around it, leaning them against the frame and the trunk of the tree. I positioned three right in front of the photo so the petals touched her shoulders and throat. The wind picked up and one of the roses leaning against the tree tipped over. I set it back in place and then removed the candles from the plastic bag and put them on the curb beside the others. The bag filled with wind and took off, floating and bouncing down the street like a little ghost.

"Here," Heidi said, giving me the book of matches.

"I think it's too windy," I said. I tugged out one of the matches and lit it. There was a small burst of fire, a moment when my fingers glowed orange before the wind swallowed the flame. "It's not going to work," I said.

Heidi sat down beside me and made a wall with her hands around one of the candles. "Try it now."

I pulled out another match and dragged it across the strike strip. Another flame burst in my hands, wavered.

By the time we finally lit the candle, three matches later, the wind snuffed it out within seconds. "I knew that was going to happen," I said.

"What should we do?" Heidi asked.

I looked across the street as if the answer were there, under the bright lights of a gas station where a woman was filling up her green sedan.

"Was she a friend of yours?" someone asked from behind, startling both of us.

He was in his mid-fifties, tall with a scraggly beard, with broad shoulders and thinning hair that the wind teased across his scalp. He wore plaid pajama bottoms and a tattered gray T-shirt with many holes.

"Yeah, she was," Heidi said.

"A good friend," I added.

"It's a shame," he said. "A damn shame. I was home when it happened." The man turned around and pointed at his house, a modest one-story with ugly lopsided bushes and a curtained window that flickered from the light of a television. "Scared me off my couch. I called

911. Took me a while to find the phone since I'd had a few."

Heidi and I both stood up and faced the man. He was barefoot and leaned too heavily on one leg, keeping his balance.

"Did you see anything?" Heidi asked.

"Lots of water. It was like one of them geysers you see on those nature programs." He made a sound then like a rocket taking off and threw his hands up in the air. He took a step back, regaining his footing. "It was amazing," he said.

I cleared my throat. "So you just stood there and watched while my friend died?"

"No, no, it wasn't like that," he said. "It wasn't like that at all. There were other people running to help. Besides, I'm not much good in situations like that. I mean, I can barely help myself." He rubbed his face with his hand, from forehead to chin, and then raised his finger. "I *did* call 911. At least I was able to do that much."

Heidi looked at the unlit candles on the curb and

then turned to the drunk man. "Do you have a lighter, by any chance?"

"Not on me," he said, patting his pajamas. "You shouldn't smoke, anyway."

"It's for the candles," I told him, but what I really felt like telling him was, *You shouldn't be a fat drunk walking around in your pajamas.*

"Oh," he said.

"We've got matches, but the wind keeps blowing them out."

"A lighter's not going to make much of a difference," he said. "Let me see one of them candles."

Heidi picked one up and handed it to the man and he brought it to his nose. "Mmmm," he said. "Smells *good.* What is that?"

"Vanilla," I said.

The man sniffed the candle again. "Va-nil-la," he said, sounding out each syllable. "That's lovely. Isn't it wonderful that there are things in this world that smell like this?" He looked at the candle and smiled as if he had found the key to happiness.

"I guess," I said.

He encircled the base of the candle with his thumb and forefinger and then handed it back to Heidi. "I'll be right back."

We watched him turn around and head toward his house, his hand held out before him as if he were still holding the candle.

"What's he doing?" Heidi asked.

"He's drunk," I said. "That's what he's doing."

"Should we go?"

"And just leave the candles here? Not even light them?"

A strand of hair flew across her mouth and she pulled it away. She set the candle back on the curb. "You want to try again?"

"Not really."

Heidi sniffled. "What's the point then?"

At the gas station across the street, the plastic bag skidded on the ground by the pumps. It stopped, twirled around in tight circles, then skidded again until it pushed itself underneath the tire of a black sports car. The headlights flashed on and the car rolled forward, flattening the bag.

"This oughta do the trick," the man said when he returned. He was holding two glasses and I thought for a moment that he'd poured us a couple drinks, something to take the edge off our grief, but then I saw the glasses were empty. "Got these at a garage sale, oh, about three or four years ago," he said. "Guy wanted thirty cents for each, but I talked him down to a dime a piece. Hand me them candles."

I grabbed the candles and held them toward the man.

"Now drop 'em in," he said.

Carefully I slipped a candle in one glass and it made a soft thud when it hit the bottom. Then I slid the other candle in the other glass and he held them both aloft, proud of himself. *"Perfect,"* he cried out.

When we attempted to light the candles again, the man stood close, blocking the wind with his body. He hovered over us and the scent of alcohol wafted from his mouth. I tipped each glass at an angle while Heidi reached in with the lit match held between two fingers.

"Bingo!" the man said.

The candles glowed a creamy light in my hands as I turned them around, examining the emblems printed on the glass. They were football helmets, washed out from numerous cycles in the dishwasher or sunlight or both. One helmet was pale green with a single wing spread across it, the other was faded blue and had a red C at its center.

"Do you need these back?" I asked the man.

"Not really," he said. "I don't care much for the Eagles, and the Bears, well, I used to love the Bears during the Perry and Payton era. Which was, what . . . two decades ago?" He open his hand and counted on his fingers. "Is that right?"

He looked at us like we would know the answer.

Heidi shrugged.

I put our candles back on the curb. "We don't follow football," I said.

"It's a great game," he said. "Brutal, poetic. You see,

187

most people think it's just barbaric. They don't see the beauty of finding the open man down the field, threading the defense with a perfect spiral. It's like an improvised ballet, you know?"

Heidi and I both nodded. She glanced at me quickly and had this let's-get-away-from-this-intoxicated-freak look on her face.

"Who knows what would've happened if I didn't blow out my knee," he said, placing his hands on his waist. "I was one of the best young quarterbacks in the country. Hell, maybe *the* best."

The man scratched his beard and waved us off and staggered back to his house mumbling to himself. He cocked his arm, then tossed an invisible football at his home. When he reached his front yard, he sat on the grass and leaned on his elbows and looked up at the dark blue of the evening.

"Let's go before he comes back," I said.

Heidi walked ahead of me. "Good idea."

We hurried to the car and jumped in, keeping our eye on the drunk man. When we pulled away he was still sitting on his lawn, looking skyward, perhaps talking to the moon. Before we turned down the street I looked back at the candles we'd left on the curb, shining brightly in each glass as if sunlight could be made into a drink.

CARLOS

In the parking lot outside the museum, I sat in my car
with my hands on the steering wheel and watched a yellow butterfly fumble around for nearly a minute—this
way, that way, spirals and loops. I listed every screwed-
up thing that had happened over the past three weeks:
Vanessa dying, Snake in a coma, Suji getting pregnant,
Mira breaking up with me, and, lastly, the asshole who'd
pissed on the museum floor on my first day at work. The
butterfly bounced around like a piece of confetti caught
above an air vent until it finally landed on the side of the

museum wall, opening and closing its wings like tiny hands clapping.

Someone rapped against the driver's-side window and I jumped in my seat. It was Nadine, the museum guard from the east wing. I caught my breath and rolled down the window.

"Sorry, I didn't mean to scare you," she said.

"It's okay," I said.

"Is everything all right?"

"Oh yeah, I'm fine." I realized that I was still holding on to the steering wheel and let go of it.

Nadine nodded like she didn't believe me. "Okay, I'll see you inside then."

I stayed in my car and watched the butterfly for a few more minutes, its wings quivering with each passing breeze. I closed my eyes and listened to the traffic on Alamitos, to the whispering of tires over pavement, how they got louder and louder as they approached the museum, then faded away down the street, like the ocean's back-and-forth with the shore.

When I stepped inside the museum, Ms. Otto was

behind the front desk, talking on the phone and writing on a notepad at the same time. "I understand," she said. "Yes, you're absolutely right." She lifted her eyes and saw me and tapped her watch with the eraser-end of her pencil. "Let me call you back. I have someone here I need to talk to."

As soon as she hung up I said, "Sorry I'm late."

"That's okay. How are you holding up?"

"So-so."

"How's your friend doing?"

"He's still in a coma."

Ms. Otto slowly shook her head. "I'm sorry." She put her palm to her forehead like she was checking if she had a fever. "I can't believe Vanessa is gone and I won't see her sweet face behind this counter again."

"I know what you mean," I said.

"Are you going to the funeral tomorrow?"

"Yeah, I'll be there. You?"

"I'm going to try to make it. I have a million things to do before next month's show. I haven't even sent out a mailing."

"Let me know if you need any help."

"Thanks, Carlos," she said. "I appreciate it."

The phone rang and Ms. Otto picked up. Her face stiffened and she slammed the phone down. "Another crank," she said.

"Maybe it's that guy who peed in the museum?" I said.

"I wouldn't be surprised." She stepped out from the front desk and headed back to her office, then quickly turned around and tore off the top sheet on the notepad beside the telephone. "Almost forgot," she said.

As I walked to my post, Leonard was staring at me with his arms folded and his head cocked at an angle. "You're late," he said flatly.

"I know, I know," I said. "My bad."

He let out a puff of air between his lips and stood up from his chair. "Some of us have shit to do. Some of us have places to be at."

"Sorry, brutha."

He laughed then, big and sarcastic. *"Sorry, brutha,"* he repeated, mocking me. *"My bad."* He placed one hand on his belly and laughed through his teeth, a hissing sound like an air pump filling a basketball.

I took Leonard's seat and felt my cheeks getting hot.

"I bet you live in a *real* nice neighborhood, in a *real* nice house," he said. "Picket fences and shit."

"We don't have fences."

"Whatever, *dawg*." He strolled away with that easy stride of his and stopped beside the rag doll Jesus. He bent down and lifted his head off the floor so the doll faced in my direction. *"My bad,"* Leonard said from the side of his mouth like a ventriloquist. He laughed some more through his teeth and walked out of the museum with his left arm swinging fluidly at his side.

I added this exchange with Leonard to my "Screwed-Up Things That Have Happened Over the Past Three Weeks" list.

I patted my coat pocket even though I knew I'd forgotten to bring my Red Vines. It wasn't long before I began chewing on my fingernails, one after the other, then spitting them out on the floor. I didn't care. I used to worry about little things like homework or zits or whether or not a person gets too close to the art pieces. Someone could've kicked the pile of green sand in the corner for all I cared. I was tempted to do it myself.

A woman walked into the museum talking loudly on her cell phone, waving one arm and saying "I know" a thousand times, with different inflections—I *know* . . . *I* know . . . *I know*—like some actor rehearsing her one line in a movie. I scowled at her. She palmed the mouthpiece and lowered her voice and kept talking, probably still repeating the same two words.

"No cell phones in the museum," I said even though I wasn't sure if that was a rule.

The woman covered the mouthpiece and turned to me. "Are you serious?"

"Yes. If you need to talk, please do it outside."

"That's crazy."

"I *know*," I said, smirking.

She squinted at me and then made her way toward the front entrance, still chattering on the phone.

A man walked in shortly after with a smug look on his face. He reeked of cologne and wore a fancy suit and fancy shoes, a large ring with a black stone on his pinkie.

Car dealer, I thought. The Mafia.

"You call this art?" he asked me.

"It is what it is," I said.

"Don't you have an opinion . . ." He leaned in close to read my name tag. "Carlos?"

"Please, step back," I said, lifting my hand up. "Your cologne's making me nauseous."

The man jerked back. His eyelids rose a fraction of an inch.

"What is that, anyway?" I said, slapping the air in front of me. "Gorilla Piss No. 5?"

The man spun around on his expensive shoes and headed toward the exit, his soles clicking fast on the hardwood floor.

Others came and went—men and women, teenagers and kids. I tried not to look angry or irritated or depressed, which made me feel even more angry, irritated, and depressed. A boy reached with his little hand toward the black painting of the war dead and his mother quickly grabbed his wrist. "You can't touch, sweetie," she said.

"Listen to your mommy," I told the boy.

The woman looked at me and pushed up a phony smile.

I showed her my teeth.

"I'm doing your job," she said, laughing nervously.

I stopped smiling. "Parenting isn't my job."

"Excuse me?"

"Never mind."

She steered her child away from the painting and together they made their way toward the exit. I waved sarcastically, my hand swinging wildly above my head like I was hailing a cab.

I laughed and laughed.

Then I thought about Snake, the soda can that held on to his shoe when he'd stomped down on it. How he'd limped across the basketball courts. How his foot had clanked with every right step.

Then my face crumpled and I cried.

I dragged my sleeve over my face and took a deep breath and sat some more, but now with the added bonus of a headache throbbing between my eyes.

* * *

My shift was almost over when Nadine walked in from the east wing of the museum. "Who knew sitting in one spot could be so exhausting," she said, yawning. "I need a coffee IV drip hooked up to my arm."

I said nothing. My head was somewhere else.

Nadine stood before Richard's neon sign, her glasses reflecting the buzzing pink words. She pulled out her ponytail and held the rubber band in her mouth, then tipped her head back and shook her blond hair loose. It swept across her shoulders like velvet gold. By the time she pulled her hair back through the O of her rubber band, I was standing beside her.

"Hey," she said.

I stared at a single blond strand swaying lazily next to her ear, above the blue shoulder of her coat.

"Your eyes look red. Have you been crying?"

"My friend's in a coma," I said.

Nadine stepped forward and gave me a hug. "I know," she said. "I'm so sorry." Her hair brushed against my cheek and smelled of honey. My arms hung limp at my sides, dead weight. Then my hands rose to her waist and I pulled her in, I tilted my head and moved my mouth over hers. Her body stiffened. She leaned back and brought her hands up to my chest, pushing me away. "What the hell are you doing?"

I looked at her shoes, the hardwood floor between them. "I wasn't . . . that wasn't . . ." I stammered.

"You can't *do* that," she said.

"I'm sorry."

"I know you're upset about your friend and all, but still."

"It's not just him," I said. "It's everything."

Nadine folded her arms. "Whatever it is, it doesn't give you license to kiss me."

"I promise it won't happen again."

"That's for damn sure." Nadine wiped her mouth and headed back to her post.

I sat back down and tried to erase what had just happened from my mind.

I patted my coat pocket again.

I chewed on my fingernails even though there wasn't much left to chew.

Soon it was seven o'clock and the sun angled its spot-light through the glass doors of the museum, illuminating the front desk. I walked through the sunlight's particles of dust, out the glass doors, into my car, and headed home—up Alamitos and down 7th, past the golf course and the Daily Grind with its large pink doughnut propped above the roof like a life preserver floating in the sky. At home I shucked off my uniform and threw on a T-shirt and jeans. I ate spaghetti and meatballs with my parents and answered their questions. *I'm okay. The funeral's tomorrow. No, I don't have to work. Yes. I haven't decided yet. They won't let me see Snake, I told you already. No, I haven't talked to her. Stop bringing her up. No thanks, I'm full.* I rinsed my plate in the sink and watched television in my room and fell asleep in the middle of *America's Most Wanted*.

I was in Ms. Wagner's health class again, sitting in the back row with Snake. The lights went out and the video came on. I turned to Snake and said, *Don't watch this.* He grinned in the blue shine of the TV. I tried to move my arms, but they were like two sandbags lying on my desk. On the screen, a man's lower leg ballooned, the skin

200

stretched and blushed to purple. *Snake*, I said. *Please don't watch*. A scalpel went through the man's leg and it popped, the skin flapped open and the bone showed itself, white as chalk. Snake toppled over, his body slammed onto the floor, the lights came on. I stood with the other students around him while Ms. Wagner caressed his forehead, then she lightly slapped his cheek, then threw a glass of water in his face, then screamed at him, then punched him in the mouth, then brought her leg back and kicked his head violently. *I guess he doesn't want to wake up*, she said. *Class dismissed*. Once we were all outside, Ms. Wagner locked the classroom door and squirted ketchup on her key and swallowed it. Minutes passed, maybe hours, maybe days. I stood at the classroom window and framed my hands around my eyes and peered in. Snake was still on the floor, but older now, with short hair and a beard and a gut, sleeping with his head on a pillow.

I woke up with the television murmuring, a snail trail of drool on my chin. According to the digital clock it was a quarter past midnight. I flipped on my computer and saw that Mira was online. My hands hovered over the keyboard and mouse for a while before I decided to send her an IM:

CarlosD: cant sleep?

I turned on my stereo and tapped the volume low and leaned back in my swivel chair, my fingers threaded behind my head, waiting for her response.

MiraGirl89: Hey, I was just thinking about you. How are you?
CarlosD: just woke up from a nightmare
MiraGirl89: I'm sorry.
CarlosD: about snake
MiraGirl89: I feel so bad for you. I know he was one of your best friends.
CarlosD: is
CarlosD: he still IS one of my best friends
MiraGirl89: That was dumb of me. I can't believe I typed that.
CarlosD: forget it
CarlosD: so how are you doing?
MiraGirl89: Okay, I guess.
MiraGirl89: Actually, not okay.

CarlosD: whats going on?

MiraGirl89: Steve made a comment about my tits being small.

CarlosD: he is already on my shit list

MiraGirl89: Like I needed to be reminded how small they are.

MiraGirl89: But that's all trivial compared to what happened this week . . . with Snake and everything.

MiraGirl89: You still there?

CarlosD: im here

MiraGirl89: How are your parents?

CarlosD: they're good. my mom asks about you every now and then

MiraGirl89: She's sweet. Tell her I said Hello. And your dad.

MiraGirl89: Hello?

CarlosD: i miss you

MiraGirl89: I miss you too.

MiraGirl89: I think about you all the time.

CarlosD: can i swing by?

CarlosD: i want to see you

MiraGirl89: Are you kidding? It's almost 12:30.

CarlosD: i know

CarlosD: i have a clock too

MiraGirl89: Smart ass. :)

CarlosD: well?

MiraGirl89: Leave in twenty minutes. I look like hell.

CarlosD: thats impossible

CarlosD: youve always looked beautiful to me

CarlosD: where did you go?

MiraGirl89: I'm crying now.

CarlosD: why?

MiraGirl89: What I did to you was so shitty. You deserve someone better than me.

CarlosD: stop it

CarlosD: im leaving in 5 minutes

MiraGirl89: Okay.

MiraGirl89: *kiss*

I knew what was going to happen before I even snuck out of my house and drove the five blocks to Mira's, before I hopped the gate like I always used to and knocked lightly on the window and climbed into her bedroom, before we talked and she cried and I stroked her hair and she tilted her wet face to mine. I knew that we would kiss, that we'd slip out of our clothes and kiss and I'd touch her and kiss and she'd moan as I went inside her, that afterward we'd lay panting, trying to catch our breath. But what I didn't expect was that I would end up feeling worse, like my heart was full of dirt and worms, and I wanted to run, put on my clothes and jump out the window and drive back home, my mind already making the trip as Mira's hand slid back and forth across my chest, my mind spinning like a carousel ride until it settled on Nadine's face, the neon pink squiggles on her glasses, her puzzled expression after I kissed her, and her question came back to me.

What the hell are you doing?

ISABEL

Sometimes I believed that all my obsessing over death had somehow caused what happened to happen. I had to keep reminding myself that I not only imagined Vanessa dying, but Heidi too, my mom and dad and little brother, everyone at Millikan, my next-door neighbors, strangers I passed on the street. From car wreck to murder (gun, knife, strangulation) to plane crash to electrocution and all the other ways listed in the "Risk of Death" chart, and in ways that were not listed—dog attack, shark attack, terrorist attack. And look at all those people. They were still breathing.

Of the hundred or so people who gathered around Vanessa's gravesite for the burial, Heidi and I stood in the outer circle. The sky was overcast and the air as still as the inside of a closet. Not even the trees moved, not one leaf.

Although I couldn't see the preacher, I could hear his words through the wall of black coats and dresses, over the sobs and whimpers. "Man hath but a short time to live and is full of misery," he said. "He cometh up and is cut down like a flower."

I thought, *A* woman *too. A woman also dies. And a girl just as she's becoming a woman.*

I looked down at my dress that my mom helped me pick out on Thursday. I looked at the handkerchief in my hands, my dad's initials stitched with green thread in one corner. He'd left it on my dresser in the morning and said I could keep it, that he had plenty more.

Heidi wept uncontrollably. She was a running faucet. I gave her the hanky and she mouthed *Thank you* before lifting the folded cloth to her face.

"O holy and merciful Savior," the preacher continued.

"Suffer us not, at our last hour, for any pains of death, to fall from thee."

A woman with a large black hat moved her head from side to side like she was looking for someone. A man glanced over his shoulder and shifted his weight. Then I smelled it, the putrid stench of a fart, like a plate of sardines lifted to my nose. I glanced over at Heidi and her face was already scrunched in disgust. She covered her nose and mouth with my dad's handkerchief and I was reminded of the footage from the brush fire a couple weeks ago, of a middle-aged man walking through the haze with a dishtowel held to his lower face.

I tried not to laugh, I really tried—I bit my lip, closed my eyes, pushed my tongue hard against the roof of my mouth. I remembered a conversation I had with Vanessa about the giggles, how one day she couldn't stop herself from laughing during a Spanish test. She had glanced up from her exam for a brief moment and saw her teacher twitching his nose spastically, his thick mustache jumping up and down. *I lost it,* Vanessa said. *I couldn't* not *laugh, you know?*

That's happened to me so many times, I told her.

Everyone was shushing me, she said. *Finally, Mr. Morales told me to please step out of the class, that I was distracting the other students. He said I could come back in and finish the test when I could control myself. But whenever I reached for the doorknob, I thought of his hopping mustache, and I'd laugh all over again.*

Imagine if you had the giggles in church, like at a wedding or baptism.

Oh my God, that would be awful. A funeral would be even worse.

You're right, I said. *That would be the absolute worst.*

And there I was, at a funeral, trying to swallow a giggle that was shimmying up my throat. My shoulders quivered, I made a strange noise in my mouth like a chair leg scraping across the floor. It was as if Vanessa were saying hello to me. Or good-bye.

"Earth to earth," the preacher said. "Ashes to ashes, dust to dust."

Then I stopped laughing and my heart felt heavy like a bag of cement. Next thing I knew I was sobbing like everyone else and Heidi was holding on to my hand.

Before long, people took turns dropping handfuls of dirt onto Vanessa's casket—her mother, her father, a brother I never knew she had, cousins and aunts and uncles I never met, some friends from Wilson High. Basically, people who knew her longer than me, which was pretty much everyone who was there. Vanessa had been in my life for only two weeks. What was I supposed to do with that?

Heidi and I were heading down the slope of the lawn, back to my car, when I saw Carlos in the cemetery parking lot talking to the woman with the large black hat. She was pinching the bridge of her nose right between her eyes like she was pushing away a headache.

"Isn't that Carlos?" Heidi asked.

"Yeah," I said. "Actually, I want to talk to him."

"Come on, Is, let's just get out of here."

I grabbed my keys from my purse and handed them to Heidi. "Wait in my car, okay?"

Heidi clicked her tongue. "This place depresses me."

"I'll just be a couple minutes."

Heidi took my keys and marched toward the car, obviously annoyed.

I stood on the sidewalk and waited for Carlos to finish his conversation. I overheard the woman say something about a mailing, about stuffing envelopes and catering and painting the walls and hiring another receptionist. I glanced up and saw Vanessa's brother walking quickly down the lawn, a lit cigarette spooling blue threads of smoke from his hand. His mother and father, their arms hooked together, trailed behind him, taking careful steps down the steep lawn. When the brother reached the sidewalk, he took one last drag from his cigarette before dropping it to the ground. He moved his shoe over it and hesitated—his foot at an angle, the smoke rising underneath—until finally he brought it down.

"Hey," Carlos said to me. "Sorry about that."

"That's okay," I said.

"That was my boss. She wants me to work even though I have the day off." He looked off to the right, up the incline, as if he was watching people coming down it.

"I haven't seen you around school," I said.

"I've been there."

"I heard Snake's still in a coma."

Carlos put his hands in his pockets and glanced the other way, over my left shoulder. "Yep."

"Have you visited him?"

"I'm not allowed. Only relatives."

He was being short with me, avoiding eye contact and fidgeting. I wondered if he was mad at me, if there was something I'd said or done that was making him act this way.

"I'm sorry," I said. "I hope he comes out of it soon."

Carlos nodded. He scratched behind his ear with one finger.

"I thought maybe we could talk about what happened," I said.

He jingled his car keys in his pocket and moved his gaze downward, at his shoes. "What's there to talk about?"

"What happened that night. Snake, Vanessa."

"Yeah? And?"

"We both lost someone."

"Snake's not dead." Carlos sighed and shook his head. "I'm tired of people talking like he is."

"Sorry, that's not what I meant."

He glanced at his watch.

"What I meant was . . ."

He began fidgeting with his keys again.

"We were there, the four of us. You and me were the last people they saw before they took off."

Carlos finally looked at my eyes.

"Where do you think they were going?"

"I don't know," Carlos said. "I really don't know."

"I haven't been able to sleep."

"Me neither."

"Sometimes I wonder what would've happened if we'd both stayed inside the car."

"But we didn't."

"I know, but if we did—"

"You can't start thinking that way," Carlos interrupted. "It doesn't do any good."

"But none of this would've happened if we'd all stuck together."

"They wanted to be alone."

I thought about not saying it, but then the words came out: "So did we."

"Look, Isabel . . ." He paused, as if he was trying to find the right words, as if they were right there on the sidewalk and all he had to do was pick them up. "My life's really complicated right now."

"Okay," I said. I watched the cars pulling out of the parking lot, some turning left onto the main street, some right. "I understand," I told him.

"Good." He glanced at his watch again. "I need to get home and get ready for work."

"I guess I'll just see you around school then?"

Carlos nodded and walked back to his car. His head was bowed at a slight angle as if he was studying his own shadow sliding in front of him like a dark fish.

A car horn blared. I recognized its sound and pitch. I turned around in time to see Heidi leaning away from the steering wheel of my car.

Once I was in the driver's seat, I let her have it.

"I can't believe you just did that," I shouted.

"Did what?"

"Honked. We're at a cemetery, Heidi. Hell-o?"

"Okay, okay, stop yelling."

I opened my purse and rummaged through it, looking for my keys. "Damn it," I muttered.

"Relax, Is." Heidi jiggled the keys in front of my face. "You gave them to me, remember?"

I swiped the keys out of her hands.

"Is everything all right?"

"No," I said. "Everything's not all right."

"What did he say?"

"I don't want to talk about it."

I put the key in the ignition and was about to turn it when Heidi said, "Why is she staring at us?"

I looked at Heidi and followed her gaze, through the windshield and over to the sidewalk where a thin girl stood in a simple black dress, facing us. Her hair was dyed platinum white and cut short like a boy's. She held her purse with both hands, then raised one tentatively.

"Do you know her?" Heidi asked.

"I don't think so."

"Are you sure?"

I turned the key halfway so the car's power came on. I lowered the window and poked my head out. "Do I know you?" I asked the girl.

She came over to the car and I realized how thin she was. She was all bones, a waif of a girl with twig arms and a scrawny neck and collarbones poking out from under her dress like a wire hanger.

"Are you Isabel?" she wanted to know.

"Yeah. Who are you?"

"I'm Sara. One of Vanessa's friends from Wilson."

"Oh," I said. "She never mentioned her friends from Wilson."

"Doesn't surprise me." She crouched and tilted her head sideways. "And you must be Heidi?"

"I am," Heidi said.

"How did you know who we were?" I asked.

"Vanessa talked about you two all the time." Sara

smiled without showing her teeth. "I knew all her friends at Wilson, so when I saw you two walking together . . . well, it didn't take a genius to figure out who you were."

Heidi leaned toward the thin girl. "What did she say? About us, I mean."

Sara slid the tip of her finger down the side of her mouth as if she was fixing her lipstick, which was a dark rose color. "Good things, mostly."

"Mostly?" I was getting angry. *Who the hell does this bony chick think she is?* I thought.

"Listen," Sara said, "Vanessa talked shit behind all her friends' backs. Even mine."

"Oh, is that right?" I said.

"You have no idea what kind of girl she was, do you?"

I remembered what Vanessa had told me on the phone one night, how she used to hang out with the wrong crowd. *Drugs and stuff. It got out of hand,* she'd told me. I began wondering if Sara was part of that crowd, if she was one of the reasons why Vanessa transferred to Millikan. I looked at Sara and said nothing.

"That's what I thought. And, actually, that's the way she wanted it."

I started the car. "It was nice meeting you," I said dryly.

I lowered the brake and checked my mirrors and began to pull out of the parking spot. Sara followed, walking casually by the driver's-side door. She had one more thing to tell me, but I was done listening to her crap and peeled out of the parking lot, the tires squealing on the pavement.

"Hell-o?" Heidi said, mocking me. *"We're at the cemetery."*

CARLOS

After the funeral, I went home and changed clothes and checked my email. There was one from Mira with the subject heading "Call me after you read this." I clicked it open and her letter filled the screen, a wall of text from one side of the monitor to the other. I didn't have time to read it, nor did I want to. Hooking up with Mira the previous night had been a mistake, plain and simple, so I deleted her email without reading it. If there was a way I could've blocked out that evening and hit the BACKSPACE button, I would've done that too.

At the museum I walked past the east wing and saw that Nadine was suited up and filing her nails, dragging the emery board casually across her fingertips. I held up my hand toward her and she kept on filing as if I didn't exist.

I knocked on Ms. Otto's office door even though it was already open. While she typed furiously at her computer, her printer was spitting out sheets of address labels. Without so much as a glance in my direction, she said, "Just give me two seconds." She was still wearing the black blouse and pants she wore to the funeral, but her large hat was nowhere to be seen.

"One . . . *two*," I said, teasing.

Ms. Otto didn't respond. She just kept typing away, mumbling the words to herself, the keyboard firecracking underneath her hands.

The stack of address labels was getting pretty thick, so I removed them from the output tray. All of a sudden the printer began chewing on a sheet. A wheel inside made a grinding noise and the ERROR light started blinking red.

"I didn't touch anything," I said, trying to look innocent, the warm stack of labels in my hands.

Ms. Otto swiveled away from her computer and rolled toward the printer. "It's been doing that," she said. "For some reason it doesn't like these address labels." She pressed a couple buttons and readjusted the blank sheets into the feeder.

"You want me to get started on something?" I asked her.

"Yes, actually." From underneath a table in the corner of her office she slid out a cardboard box stuffed with sealed envelopes. The museum's logo—the letters LBCM floating in a red square—was printed in the corner of each envelope. "You can start by putting labels on these," she said.

"No problem."

She wheeled back to her computer using her feet. "Make yourself comfortable."

I placed the labels on top of the envelopes and moved the box to the glass coffee table. Her couch was sleek in design and made of leather the color of dark chocolate. I sat down and began to unpeel the address labels, sticking them to the envelopes as straight and dead-center as I could. Five minutes into it, Ms. Otto turned around and said, "How are we doing?"

I was aligning a label just right. "Good."

"It doesn't have to be perfect, Carlos. It just has to get there, you know?"

"Sorry."

"That's okay. There's just lots to do," she said. "When you're done with those, I've got some postcards for next month's exhibit that also need labels."

Ms. Otto went back to whatever she was working on and I picked up my pace with the labeling until I had a steady rhythm going, the envelopes moving from one hand to the next before I dropped them into the cardboard box. I was like a factory machine. *Peel, stick, drop. Peel, stick, drop.* I was certain there wasn't a faster labeler in all of Long Beach.

My mind wandered and I thought about Mira, the email I deleted.

Peel, stick, drop.

I thought about Snake. The dream. Ms. Wagner kicking his head.

Peel, stick, drop.

Isabel and the way I left her at the cemetery parking lot.

Peel, stick, drop.

How guilty I felt for hooking up with Mira when I had no intention of getting back with her.

Peel, stick, drop.

How afraid I was that Isabel would see the guilt on my face.

For a half hour straight I labeled, barely even reading the names, but there was one I paused on: Richard Spurgeon. His address label stuck to my fingertip like an unpeeled Band-Aid. I decided to say his name out loud to test my theory that he and Ms. Otto had once been together.

"Rich-ard Spur-geon," I said slowly. "Isn't that the neon artist guy?"

Ms. Otto swiveled around in her chair. "Give me

223

that." She stuck her hand out. "He won't be in town for the opening." She plucked the label from my fingertip and crumpled it in her hand.

"I thought the postcards were for the opening?"

"Yes, well . . ." She paused and motioned toward the box of envelopes. "Those are letters asking for donations. I generally don't like to ask artists for money."

"Oh," I said. "I see."

The printer began crunching on another sheet. Ms. Otto made a growling noise with her teeth clenched and rolled her chair over and pulled the ruined labels out.

"Are you friends with him?" I asked.

"Acquaintances," she said, rolling back to her computer.

"He seems like a nice guy. I had to help him move the sign to his car. He acted like—"

"Carlos," she interrupted. "I need to finish typing this letter."

"Sorry."

Peel, stick, drop.

We worked together for a good hour in silence except

for Ms. Otto's occasional mumbling. Once I finished labeling the envelopes, I moved on to the postcards that announced the new exhibit in three weeks. The postcards had a photograph of a red balloon lying on its side in the grass. Because the picture was taken from a low angle, you could see the blurry background in what appeared to be a park, the green splotches of trees under a blue sky, an unfocused man or woman walking down a fuzzy pathway. Tethered with a piece of string to the balloon's navel was a card like the ones coroners slip on a dead person's toe. On the card there were five lines—one for NAME, one for AGE, three for WISH—that someone had already filled out with a blue felt-tip pen, too messy to read.

Ms. Otto kept mumbling to herself while she typed. The printer continued to jam on the address labels until I clasped two fat binder clips on both sides of the feeder, forcing the sheets to go down straight. "How ingenious," Ms. Otto said.

Again my thoughts wandered to Isabel, to Mira and Snake and then back to Isabel, what she said in the parking lot back at the cemetery. *We were there, the four of us. . . . Where do you think they were going? . . . none of this would've happened if we'd all stuck together.* Although I told her thinking that way was pointless and wouldn't change anything, I had the same thoughts and often had an alternate version of the evening playing in my head. I don't open my mouth and say, *Let's go inside and tear up the dance floor,* I don't open the car door, I don't tell Isabel to come with me. Instead, the four of us sit together in the car, drinking and laughing, until Snake pulls the key out of the ignition and says, *Come on, let's show off our moves,* and we all stumble out into the cool evening and cross the parking lot, take our raffle tickets outside the gymnasium entrance, and step into the blaring music and flashing lights and dance.

Around three o'clock I was all done with the labeling. I stood up from the couch and twisted at the waist, cracking my back. Ms. Otto thanked me for coming in on my day off and said I could go home. "See you tomorrow," she said.

"*Tuesday,*" I corrected her.

"That's right." She jerked her head like a bug had

226

flown into her hair. "I can't get my days straight. There's too much going on right now."

"I know," I said. "I feel the same way."

"At least you know what day it is."

I smiled and walked out of her office. I waved good-bye to Bridget at the front desk, who was laughing on the phone, obviously talking to someone she knew.

Just outside the museum I found Nadine sitting on a concrete bench, smoking. She leaned forward and looked down like someone sitting at the end of a pier, watching the blue water below.

"Bye," I said weakly.

Nadine wouldn't look at me.

I followed the pathway through the grass, feeling really small, and imagined myself the size of an action figure, scaling up the abstract sculpture in front of the museum like a man climbing a high-rise from the future. Nadine called my name and I turned around and watched her tap out her cigarette on the side of the bench. "Get over here," she said.

I walked back, my hands in my pockets, head lowered,

so she knew how sorry I felt for kissing her before I apologized again. "I'm really sorry about yesterday," I told her.

"Forget about it," she said. "Water under the bridge."

"I don't know what came over me."

"Stupidity." Nadine smirked.

"Okay, I guess I deserved that." I sat down beside her on the bench, but not too close.

"I didn't call you over to badger you. I wanted to ask a favor."

"Shoot."

"Could you cover my shift tomorrow?"

I made a face that said, *Oh no, don't ask me to do that.*

"You know . . ." she began. "What you did yesterday was *really* inappropriate."

I smiled. "Okay, okay, I get it."

"So is that a yes?"

"Yes," I said.

"Thanks, Carlos. I'll let Ms. Otto know."

I stood up from the bench. "Okay, now it's *my* turn to ask *you* for a favor."

She raised her eyebrows. "Oh, yeah? What is it?"

"No more using what I did yesterday to guilt me into covering your shifts."

Nadine stuck out her hand. "Deal."

ISABEL

Go back. All I wanted to do was go back and undo everything that had happened over the past year. Just rewind and erase, rewind and erase, until my heart was repaired and I could trust the world again. . . .

The mourners walk backward, their legs jerking up the slope of the lawn toward Vanessa's gravesite. At the bottom of the hill, Vanessa's brother raises his foot off the ground and a cigarette leaps up, wedging itself between his fingers. Then he too walks backward up the lawn, his parents trailing behind him—all three of them pulled closer and closer to where the dirt is flying out of the open grave and into the mourners' hands. "Dust to dust," the preacher says. "Ashes to ashes, earth to earth."

Heidi takes the flame away from the candle's wick and back onto the tip of a match head. I hold my hand over the glass and the candle slides up to my fingers. Across the street, a black sports car rolls in reverse into a gas station. A plastic bag on the pavement inflates as the tire rolls over it, then the bag spirals away. Wind breathes a flame into a burnt-out match I'm holding in my hand. I look at the ruined wall and Snake's car pulls away from it, the bricks rising back in place.

A heart cut from construction paper hops off the gymnasium floor and slips between the double doors just as Carlos closes them. We walk into the crowd, hand in hand. A red balloon floats to his head and swerves quickly into my slap. We dance, then move away from the flailing crowd, the warm air leaving our bodies as we step outside. We return our raffle tickets to Ms. Lauden, Mr. Bissell erases two marks on a sheet with the tip of a pencil. We zigzag through the parking lot all the way to Snake's car. Carlos sucks air out of his cupped hands and then rubs them together. I climb into the backseat and see Vanessa's blue profile in the console's glow. Her hand is over my hand. My hand is on her shoulder, unsqueezing it gently.

Bite by bite I piece the licorice together and hand it to Carlos. He pushes the licorice into its bag, slips it into his jacket pocket, asks me if I want a Red Vine. Around the middle of the room I linger, wishing Carlos would talk to me. Heidi steps away from the pile of green sand and points at the pink neon sign on the wall. I take strands of hair from behind my ear, pull them forward so they rest alongside my cheek. I read the overlapping names on the black painting. When I step away from it, the names sink into the canvas.

The tail of a lizard dangles from Roland's raised fist as he tiptoes into the flower beds, turns, and lifts his empty hands from behind the quivering daisies. The smell of burning trees blows away from me as I close the sliding glass door. I sit on the couch where Vanessa and Heidi pull wedges out of their mouths and fit them into their oranges. I motion toward the tree in our yard. Vanessa mends the peeled skin over her fruit. Above Heidi's hands, a cloud of mist forms like a ghost and disappears into her orange. It's the one-year anniversary of Gabriel's passing.

I sob in the shower, the water leaping from my body and shooting into the showerhead. I get dressed and go to my room where the "Risk of Death" chart, crumpled in a ball, springs out of the wastebasket and into my hand. I stretch out my fingers and the clipping flattens out. In the kitchen, my dad walks in from the garage and places a banana in the fruit bowl, twisting it at the stem until it joins the bunch. Mom tells him to take a banana. He says good-bye to us and hurries to the bedroom. I look at the clipping and notice there are many ways to die that aren't included on the chart. The microwave beeps, then glows a dull yellow behind the glass where Roland's frozen pancakes turn counterclockwise, getting colder and colder.

The weeks reel back, the months—September, August, July, June. My mind is nowhere and elsewhere at once. The ache

233

grows inside my chest as May turns to April, March to February. Tears crawl into my eyes more and more—at home, during class, under bedcovers, in the shower. The grief sharpens, then the shock of the phone call: Gabriel is dead. The telephone rings.

His car emerges out of the glittering blue canal, water materializing out of the air and into a giant splash folding into itself. The car rolls up the embankment and the chain-link fence rises as he crashes out of it. The car hops down the curb, skids out of a turn, accelerates. Backward he drives toward my house and I watch him coming down my street. I taste the spearmint of his gum, I lean into his lips, he leans into mine, and we unkiss.

CARLOS

The days moved slow and fast at once, like a dream of standing in place while the world reeled in front of my eyes. At the museum it slowed when the pieces were unplugged, taken down, dismantled, carted off, and slowed again when two men slipped the rag doll Jesus into a giant plastic bag, carried him to the parking lot where the artist waited in his truck. In Spanish another two men spoke while they shoveled the large pile of green sand into a wheelbarrow, then swept, then vacuumed. The chest of the sleeping museum guard stopped moving up and down, his cord yanked from the wall socket. And then Richard Spurgeon arrived with a paint-spattered black T that looked like he was wearing a galaxy, with the same yellow blanket folded under his arm, and together we transported his neon sign once more to his car minus the ash floating into my eye. He started the engine and I motioned for him to roll down the car window and when he did, half the sky disappeared in the glass, and I asked him flat-out if he used to date Ms. Otto, and he gave me this big shit-eating grin and said, *Not sure if I would use the word "date."* The minutes hovered, fell, rose, and through the museum entrance arrived the artist who made the self-portrait entirely out of wads of bubble gum, and I asked if she'd heard about the boy in Detroit who pressed his gum onto a painting worth $1.5 million, and she laughed and said, *I'm glad no one did that to mine,* and I said, *How would you know?* I was there when the two televisions facing each other were unplugged, and Nadine was there too, and when the artist was out of earshot (a shy man in corduroys and a plaid shirt), she said, *Thank God I don't have to hear that again,* so I kept repeating the video's looped message—*My starling . . . Come back . . . The key is under the doormat . . . My starling . . . Come back*—until Nadine threatened to strangle me with the Red Vine I was chewing on. I laughed, it might've looked like I was doing okay, but in the back of my mind I was always thinking about Snake—his face, his voice, his face, his laugh, his face—and finally one day after work I drove to the hospital, went up the elevator to the Trauma Center, and told the woman in a yellow shirt behind the counter that Jeffrey McKenzie was my friend, one of my best, that I wanted to see him. The world paused. Then a woman in a white jacket came and down the hallways I followed her as her white tennis shoes moaned softly with each footstep. It killed me when I first saw him, his closed eyes, his head still swollen and faintly bruised from the accident, a watercolor of pale green and yellow clouds on his cheek and forehead, the valleys of his sockets. His lips were chapped and his mouth was partially open as if he was about to speak, but I did all the talking and scooted a chair by his bed and said, *Hey,* and said, *I know you're going to come out of this thing,* and said, *Pretty soon it'll be the three of us again on the bleachers.*

You, me, and Will. For a good ten minutes I talked to him and said nothing with him for another ten and left weeping and ruined, left wishing he'd just wake up and get back on his feet so we could hang out again, so we could laugh and talk about stupid shit like whether or not it's better to use dolphins or carrier pigeons instead of puppies to smuggle in heroin from Mexico. The world stalled, lurched forward, its mosaic of colors, its elaborate sound track. Behind my desk I sat, half listening to Mr. Hunnicutt's lecture on the Great Depression, and then the room changed, the configuration of desks, and I was in Ms. Vann's class, doodling geometric shapes on my notebook as she talked about *The Red Badge of Courage,* the epiphany Henry Fleming had with the squirrel in the woods, and I thought, *Screw the squirrel—my friend's in a coma.* So it was mostly me and Will on the bleachers, a herd of clouds stampeding silently across the sky, and sometimes this scrawny kid named Eric Fontaine joined us, a freshman who talked incessantly about all the girls he nailed at DeMille Junior High and all the girls he was going to nail at Millikan. We egged him on, Will and me, and laughed at the absurdity of his accounts, our sides aching, tears sliding down our cheeks, *I had her feet on my shoulders like this,* Eric said, demonstrating with his hands curled beside his neck. But usually it was just me and Will in the bleachers, and a few seagulls milling around the basketball courts, and on those days we talked about Snake (still in a coma after two and a half weeks) and Suji (whom I saw at Millikan every now and then, cheerless, slow-footed, her head bowed like a wounded animal) and the shittiness of life in general. I avoided both Mira and Isabel on campus, I scanned the quad before crossing it, I turned corners anxiously. Still, Mira called and sent me emails, some I deleted and some I read, a handful of sentences or long-winded letters filled with words like *love* and *us* and *hiding*, until finally she sent an email with only one word: *coward.* Will tried desperately to get in touch with Suji (on campus, by phone, by email) to say how sorry he was, to explain himself, but Suji would have none of it and sent him a text message that said *Leave me alone,* which he did, which drove him nuts—his clothes became more wrinkled, his hair more oily. Like a dream, the world rolled in front of me, shadowy and dazzling. Back at the museum, workers spackled over the holes and repainted the walls white, their paint-speckled boots echoing throughout the empty museum, and so for two weeks while the exhibits changed over I was off from work, two weeks without Ms. Otto, Nadine, Leonard, or Bridget, my uniform hanging inside my closet like a giant bat, and with my extra time I caught up with homework, I cleaned my room and watched television mindlessly, and read articles about comas on the internet, the persistent vegetative state that sometimes follows, about falling into a deep state of unconsciousness simply by drinking too much, that silent abyss, and I remembered all the times that Snake and Will and me pounded beers at some party, how wasted we got, how unbalanced, and the night a girl came up to us with vomit in her hair, weaving, slurring, asking us if we could take her home, and we steered her instead toward the chaise lounge by the swimming pool and left her there by the lapping water, alone, like a patient in a hospital bed. I dreamed Mira gave me a blow job at a graveyard. I dreamed Snake was a museum guard sleeping in his chair until someone came and took him apart, wires dangling from his hollow torso like black spaghetti. I dreamed of Isabel's face—smooth, egg-shaped, radiant, her eyes green and caring—and at school the next day I scanned the quad again, looking for that face, that wavy dark hair, and when I couldn't find her I went to the cafeteria, to the administration building, to the concrete steps outside the theater building, wind blowing through the nearby trees, its leaves silently clapping. Down the halls I strolled, looking, looking, until I spotted Isabel coming out of the girls' bathroom with her friend Heidi, both of them chattering away until Isabel saw me, then a silence filled the hallway and hardened like glue, so the three of us were frozen there, our words caught in our throats, and then I said, *Can I talk to you for a second?* and Isabel said, *Yes,* and Heidi said, *I'll meet you by the planters.* And once we were alone, I apologized for avoiding her, for the way I'd acted at Vanessa's funeral, how unsympathetic I'd been, my hands fidgeting, *You'd just said good-bye to your friend,* I told her, *and then you had me afterward, acting like an asshole.* She smiled, her eyes shimmering like green tinsel, and she asked if my life was still too complicated right now, throwing my words back at my face. I winced, fidgeted, and said, *Did I really say that?* and she nodded and I said, *No, it's not too complicated for you.* I dug into my backpack then and took out the glossy postcard for the opening at the museum on Saturday and handed it to Isabel and told her she should go, free drinks and food, that the exhibit was interactive, how fun it would be. She slipped the postcard into her purse and said, *If my life's not too complicated on Saturday, I'll go.* And then the world moved leisurely again, the seconds dripped like honey, and as Isabel walked away down the hall—that tunnel of lockers and corkboard and Xeroxed flyers—her hair sailed like a dream over her shoulder blades, so slow and vivid I could've counted each delicate strand.

ISABEL

Heidi promised she'd go to the art opening even though she said she could think of a hundred other things to do on a Saturday night that were less painful and began listing them. Root canal, high school play, laundry, any movie starring Bruce Willis. I stopped her after she said bowling. *Nothing's more painful than bowling,* I told her.

We drove in silence for a while, staring out through the windshield at the traffic, all those taillights shining red before us like radiant hearts.

Heidi turned to me. "You look cute, by the way," she said.

I was wearing a dark green dress, my favorite black sweater with the pearly buttons. Heidi was in a red skirt printed with black flowers, very Spanish, and a simple white top.

"You do too," I said. "Too bad Matt Hawkins can't see you now."

"No kidding!"

"You'd turn his head. And that's a lot of head to turn."

"Ah, leave his poor forehead alone," she whined.

At a traffic light, I glanced up at an apartment building and saw a woman framed by a window. She was holding a phone with one hand, sipping from a wineglass with the other.

"So do you really like this Carlos guy or what?" Heidi asked.

"Yeah, I think so," I said. "It's sort of hard to tell. My emotions have been all over the place. First it was Gabriel's anniversary, then Vanessa . . ."

"I know what you mean." Heidi turned down Alamitos and flicked on her headlights. "It's like your heart finally healed just before it got broken again."

"Exactly."

"Just let things happen with Carlos. Don't force anything."

"That's what I'm planning on doing," I said.

We pulled into the parking lot and cruised up and down the rows until we found a spot. We stepped out and there was a nice breeze with the faintest scent of the ocean in it. The curved pathway to the front entrance was lined on both sides with tiny lights, reminding me of the aisles in a movie theater.

When we stepped into the museum there was this hum of excitement, the sound of conversations overlapping, the squeal of laughter. I held Heidi's hand and together we slowly pushed through the crowd, my eyes jumping around, looking for Carlos. There were lots of suits and ties, dresses and jewelry. Everyone looked stylish except for a handful of art punks in jeans and T-shirts with oily hair and multiple piercings. I got the impression that *this* was the place to be. And we were there.

Some people were holding clear plastic cups of wine and I motioned to Heidi with my hand to my mouth. She nodded and I plowed through—*Excuse me, excuse me*—until we were standing before a table covered with hors d'oeuvres: a cheese plate and a fan of crackers, carrot sticks and celery sticks, olives, grapes, miniature muffins, and these meatball-looking things skewered with colored toothpicks. We scooted over to the next table where a man in a white waiter's jacket and black tie stood with his hands behind his back. About a dozen unopened bottles of wine crowded one side of the table. I held up two fingers.

"Can I see some ID?" the man said.

I frowned.

"Aw, come on," Heidi pleaded.

"We also have club soda and bottled water," he offered.

"Forget it." Heidi grabbed my hand and pulled me away from the table.

We were standing near a wall beside a large photograph of a silver-haired man blowing air into a red balloon, cheeks puffed, his hand wrinkled and age-spotted. "We need to find someone to get us drinks," Heidi said.

"Who?" I said. "We don't know anyone here."

"Where's your boyfriend, anyway?" Heidi teased.

"He's not my boyfriend."

"Yet."

I shot her a look. "What happened to letting this happen and not forcing things?"

Heidi pointed. "There he is."

I followed the imaginary line that extended from her fingertip across the room and spotted Carlos in a green button-up shirt tucked into black jeans, the sleeves rolled to his elbows. He was talking to a blond woman with glasses, a cup of wine sloshing in her hand. She was all smiles, standing close to Carlos.

"Uh-oh," Heidi said. "Looks like someone's got her eye on your boyfriend."

"Shut up," I said.

"Quick, do something."

"She's, like, *thirty-five*."

The woman leaned closer. Carlos straightened his

back and turned his head to the side.

"Oh my *God*!" Heidi exclaimed. "She *so* wants to kiss him."

There was no denying it. The woman—whoever she was, however old, however drunk—wanted Carlos's lips. And he wasn't giving them to her.

Heidi nudged my elbow. "Are you going to let her steal your man?"

"Don't be silly," I said. "No one's stealing anyone from anyone."

A couple crossed in front of us, blocking my view—the woman in a shawl pointing at a photograph, the man saying something into her ear—and then they were out of my line of vision. The blonde had her hand clamped on Carlos's jaw like a chin strap, directing his mouth toward hers, kissing him.

"See," Heidi said. *"I told you."*

The blonde let go of Carlos's face and pushed up her glasses, drained her cup and handed it to him, then walked away, her shoulders thrown back. Carlos looked around the room to see if anyone had seen what happened.

I know it's dumb, but I was a little jealous at that moment. I felt it in my heart, this little pinch.

I zoned out, the room squeezed into a glass tunnel, but before I could imagine everyone around me dropping dead, Carlos swept his hand back and forth in front of my eyes like a windshield wiper. "Anyone home?"

"I'm sorry," I said, shaking my head, embarrassed.

"She does that all the time," Heidi said.

"Not *all* the time."

"More than any normal person should."

I elbowed Heidi.

"What time did you guys get here?" Carlos asked.

"About ten, fifteen—"

"Who was that woman?" Heidi said, cutting me off.

I elbowed her again.

Carlos blushed. "Oh no, you saw that?" He was looking right at me.

"Sort of," I said.

"She's really drunk," he said. "I work with her. She's a museum guard too."

"She's a little old for you, don't you think?" Heidi said.

"Like I said, she's really drunk."

I giggled, but I was still jealous. There was still a little pinch.

Carlos leaned close to my ear. "I'm glad you decided to come."

"Me too," I said, smiling.

"Did you guys do a balloon yet?" Carlos asked.

I had no idea what he was talking about. I looked at Heidi. She didn't seem to either.

"Come on," he said, grabbing my hand. "You have to do this."

CARLOS

It was a daring move, grabbing Isabel's hand and making my way through the crowd, but I was full of confidence. Maybe it was Nadine's drunken kiss that made me so self-assured. Maybe I was tired of taking things for granted and floating through my life like a windblown candy wrapper. Whatever it was, I held tight to Isabel's hand and together we headed to the east wing of the museum.

On the way over, I spotted Richard Spurgeon talking to Ms. Otto, her hand fiddling with an earring. I had intentionally stuck his address label on a postcard, knowing there might be trouble if he showed up. But there they were, chatting away, no trouble at all. Richard caught my eye and winked. I gave him a thumbs-up.

I brought Isabel and Heidi to the circular wall of Plexiglas that was the centerpiece of the east wing. The Plexiglas was knee-high and within its transparent barricade were all the tagged red balloons, hundreds of them, each filled with a different person's breath. All the ceiling lights were aimed inside the wall, spotlighting the balloons, and their tight red skins held on to the light. The whole thing looked like the cross section of a pomegranate.

"I don't get it," Heidi said.

"What does it say on the cards?" Isabel asked.

"They're people's wishes," I said. "You blow up a balloon and then fill out this card with your name and age and wish." I held on to Isabel's arm. "Get closer," I said, crouching.

Isabel bent down so we were both sitting on the heels of our feet. I pointed at the nearest balloon with its card facing up, and she placed her hand on my shoulder for balance. "I can't read it from here."

"I'll tell you," I said. "It says . . . 'Henry Gibson . . . age forty-six' . . . and his wish is . . ." I inched closer, my knees practically touching the wall. ". . . 'My treatment works and I have many years to live with my family.'"

Isabel made a small moaning sound. "That's so sad."

"Yeah, some of them are," I said. "But some are funny. I read one earlier that said 'I wish to lose my *virgin* soon.'"

Isabel laughed.

"The kid was only eleven."

"Whoa, slow down, Billy," she said.

I looked across at all the other balloons. They reminded me of large, red lightbulbs. A woman on the far end was also crouching as she held her curly blond hair away from her face. She was reading the cards one after another. She smiled, she frowned, she bit her bottom lip, she laughed, covering her mouth, then she frowned again.

Isabel and I stood up and a balloon sailed over our heads. It dropped lazily in front of us, the card twirling at the end of its string. Isabel turned around.

"Somebody made a wish," I said.

"*I want to make one,*" Heidi said, all excited, like a child.

"We have to go over there," I said, pointing toward a mob of people.

Heidi turned around and wiggled her way through the crowd. Isabel and I followed. This time, *she* was tugging me along, squeezing my hand and leading the way.

I spotted Leonard, dressed in a maroon blazer and black shirt. He was talking to a lovely woman in a metallic green dress, her hair all done up, tight curls spiraling down her cheeks. Our eyes met, Leonard's and mine, and he jerked his head faintly in my direction. The Monday after he had chewed me out for being late for work, he'd apologized, blaming his mood on an argument he'd had with his girlfriend. We'd tapped our fists together and nothing more was said about the incident.

We scooted through the horde of jackets and blouses like penguins. Eventually the three of us made it to the front of the table where a large crystal bowl held a mound of uninflated balloons. A smaller bowl held the blank cards, the strings already tied to them. There were two cups, one on each end of the table, crammed with pens. The tablecloth was made of white silk and had Japanese characters sewn into the shiny fabric. On one side there was an intricate embroidery of a cherry blossom tree in full bloom. Underneath its branches, a woman in a turquoise kimono was watching the pink flowers floating in a pond, a serene smile stitched on her face.

Heidi grabbed one of the cards and plucked a pen from a cup, her tongue poking out of the corner of her mouth as she wrote.

A woman standing beside me blew into a balloon and it expanded in front of her face like bubble gum.

Isabel leaned over Heidi's shoulder. "What's your wish?"

Heidi slapped her hand over her card. *"Don't look,"* she said. "It's a secret."

"I bet I could guess," Isabel teased.

"I bet I know what yours will say," Heidi shot back.

"Are you going to do one?" I asked Isabel.

She shook her head no. "I'll do one later."

"I promise I won't look," I reassured her.

She smiled and shook her head again.

Heidi snatched a balloon from the crystal bowl and put it to her lips. She blew until the balloon was the size of a watermelon.

"That's good," Isabel said.

Heidi pulled the balloon from her mouth, pinching the end closed. She blinked hard. "I'm all light-headed now," she said. *"Whew."*

I held my hand out. "Want me to tie it?"

Heidi gave me her balloon and I pulled the end around my finger like a rubber band, then looped it under and made a knot. I handed the balloon back to Heidi. "There you go."

Heidi tied the card to her balloon and then we were following her through the crowd until we were in the east wing again, standing beside the Plexiglas wall. A man with dreadlocks held a balloon up high like a heart at a sacrificial ceremony. Heidi lifted her balloon and tossed it in with the others.

I tapped Isabel's shoulder. "Are you glad you came?"

"Yes," she said. "Heidi wasn't nuts about coming, but look at her now." Isabel flapped her hand in front of her face.

"You want to get some air?" I asked.

"Yeah," she said. "It's hot in here with all these people."

"I'm going to make another wish," Heidi said. "I'll catch up with you guys later."

The night air cooled our faces while we sat on one of the concrete benches just outside the entrance. Stars made little pinholes of light above us. Three men in suits stood on the grass, one waving a lit cigarette around as he told a story. I had grabbed an Evian from the waiter before we stepped out and we now drank from it, passing the water back and forth, the mouth of the bottle stained crimson from Isabel's lipstick.

We talked for an hour straight, maybe longer—about our families and childhood memories, our birthdays and zodiac signs. We talked about Millikan, Red Vines, the White Stripes, Charlie Kaufman, and frozen yogurt. Snake was on my mind, and I'm sure Vanessa was on hers, but we didn't bring them up. Not yet.

Isabel finished the water and handed me the empty bottle.

"Gee, thanks," I said, sarcastic.

"You're welcome."

"Want me to run in and get another?"

"No," she said. "Stay here."

There was a long pause.

"I wonder what Heidi's doing," I said.

"She's probably chasing some guy around." She did that goofy chipmunk smile thing, really fast—a nervous twitch but cute nonetheless.

There was another long pause.

Isabel looked at the cars on Alamitos, driving through the night. I wanted to kiss her, but the confidence I'd had earlier was gone. I was shy, nervous, uncomfortable in my skin. Butterflies—no, *bats*—fluttered around inside my stomach.

An older couple walked out of the museum, arm-in-arm, smiling, and the man nodded at us.

"Good night," Isabel said.

I waved to the couple.

"Good night," the woman said.

The couple continued on down the pathway that was outlined with strings of lights. Then we were alone again, quiet again, the moon playing peekaboo behind a tree branch.

I told myself, *I'll kiss her the next time a couple walks out of the museum.*

A man in a brown suit stepped out, a cell phone pressed to his ear.

I revised my promise: *I'll kiss her the next time* anyone *walks out of the museum.*

I looked at Isabel and smiled.

She smiled back and lifted her eyebrows.

"We're all talked out," I said.

"Yes," she said. "We're done talking."

I watched the museum entrance, waiting for the next person to step out. Through the glass doors, above the crowd, between two walls, a red balloon had been lobbed into the air and floated down like a time-lapse video of a sunset.

Isabel grabbed my chin and turned my head. We kissed. I let go of the empty water bottle and put my hand on her knee. Our tongues rolled around, lazily, clockwise. I opened my eyes quickly to see if she was looking, and her eyes were shut, the lashes folded down. We kissed some more and then she put her hand lightly on my chest and backed away.

"That was nice," she said.

"Very nice," I added.

"I got tired of waiting for you to kiss me."

"Sorry. I was waiting for the right moment."

"That was five minutes ago." She wiped my bottom lip with the side of her thumb. "Got lipstick on you."

"It's not my color?"

"Nope," she said. "But I've got this bright red tube at home with your name on it."

We laughed. Everything was perfect.

A man wearing a mechanic's jump suit was coming down the pathway at a quick pace, heading toward the museum. He looked familiar. His face. The goatee. The slender nose. I stared at him, trying to piece it all together.

"What is it?" Isabel asked.

"That guy," I said. "I know him."

She turned and looked.

Then it hit me. It was the man who had peed on the museum floor on my first day at work.

"What does he have on his shoes?" Isabel asked.

There were metal points that extended out from the tips of his boots. They looked like steak knives, and they made a *tsk-tsk* sound as he walked.

"Are those blades?" Isabel whispered.

I had to do something.

"Hey!" I shouted. *"Stop."*

He didn't stop. The glass doors glided open and he walked in.

"I have to tell Ms. Otto," I said, panicked. "Come on, let's go."

We rushed into the museum, into the warm air and chatter, the high squeal of drunken laughter. My eyes bounced around the crowd like a frightened parent looking for his child. I threaded my body around elbows, between couples, apologizing, Isabel trailing behind. I heard a man say the 5 was the worst freeway in Southern California. A plastic cup crumpled under my foot. A woman asked another woman if she'd tried the Brie. A balloon sailed overhead, its card spinning.

I spotted Richard Spurgeon and made my way toward him. Ms. Otto was nowhere around.

"Richard," I yelled.

"Hey," he said. "Carlos, right?"

"Where's Ms. Otto?" I was on edge.

"What's going on?" he asked. His hair stuck out from the sides of his head as if he'd been wrestling.

"This guy pissed on the floor and he's here now."

"Again?"

"No," I said, flustered. "That was a long time ago, but he's here now and he's got these knives or something on his shoes."

"I think they *are* knives," Isabel said.

"I need to find Ms. Otto," I told Richard.

"Janet is . . ." He paused and turned toward the short hallway that led to her office. "Is this an emergency?"

"Yes."

"Stay here," he said, his hand on my shoulder. "Let me go get her."

Richard headed toward Ms. Otto's office, zigzagging through the crowd.

I looked at Isabel.

"Feel my heart," she said. "It's beating fast."

I did. It was.

That's when we heard the first balloon pop. Then another. Then a succession of pops like Chinese firecrackers going off.

Fear rippled through the museum as everyone turned to face the commotion, their cups frozen in their hands.

"Somebody stop him!" a man shouted.

I drove forward through the crowd. *I* was that somebody who was going to stop him. "Move, move," I said to those around me. "I'm the museum guard."

More balloons burst like gunshots. People were yelling. I thought my heart was going to jump out of my mouth. Nonetheless, I pushed through, determined. My confidence was back.

By the time I reached the wall of Plexiglas, it was too late. The man in the jumpsuit was already on the ground, in a headlock. I looked closer and realized it was Leonard, still in his maroon blazer, restraining the man. He held him tight, but the man's legs scissored wildly, popping more balloons.

"Watch out for his feet!" a woman hollered.

I knew what I had to do. I took a deep breath, hopped the wall, and rushed over to help Leonard, balloons leaping around my knees.

The man's face was scarlet, his teeth clenched. I positioned myself and then fell on his legs, sitting on them. I looped my arm underneath the man's legs and clamped my hands together.

"Yo, my man Carlos," Leonard grunted. "You're late *again*."

I was terrified, but I couldn't help but laugh then.

"Get off me," the man hissed. *"Get off."*

Balloons wobbled and bounced around the three of us

like red blood cells under a microscope.

"Somebody call the cops," Leonard said calmly, as if he were ordering a dish from a menu.

Then all the cell phones came out, their tiny blue screens lighting up around us.

ISABEL

On Sunday, the day after the opening, I took the "Risk of Death" chart from my purse and tossed it in the trash. It had been silly of me to carry it around to begin with. Who needs to be reminded of all the ways you could die? I carried another clipping now, a small story I cut out of the *Press-Telegram*. The headline read: "Museum Guards Stop Art Vandal."

It was one in the afternoon when I pulled into the museum parking lot. There was a news van parked along the curb, its satellite dish angled toward a cloudless blue sky. Carlos wasn't even supposed to be working, but Ms. Otto wanted him to come in and be interviewed by the news media. Despite what had happened, she said it was excellent publicity for the museum.

When I stepped into the museum, the girl behind the counter held her finger to her lips. She motioned with her head and I looked across the room. A newswoman with poofy hair was interviewing Leonard and Carlos while a man pointed a video camera over her shoulder. Leonard was dressed in his museum guard uniform, but Carlos wore a plaid button-up shirt, faded jeans, and tennis shoes. The newswoman brought the microphone to her mouth and then to Leonard's mouth, then over to Carlos's, like the three of them were sharing an ice-cream cone.

"You heard what happened?" the girl behind the counter whispered.

"I was here," I whispered back. "I saw everything."

I passed the time by looking at the large photographs in the west wing of the museum, five to each wall. My favorite one was of an Asian girl in a yellow sundress and sandals. She was laughing, holding her red balloon up to her face, the air rushing out and pushing up her bangs.

The news crew left with their cords trailing behind them. I walked up to Carlos. He was beaming. "You're famous," I said.

"I didn't do anything," he said. "It was all Leonard."

Right when he said that, Leonard patted Carlos's back on his way over to the east wing. "Ms. Otto should give us a bonus."

"No kidding," Carlos said, chuckling.

"You held that guy's legs," I reminded him. "You stopped him from popping more balloons."

"Yeah, I guess I did," he said.

Ms. Otto came up to us and Carlos introduced me. We shook hands. Ms. Otto thanked Carlos for coming in on his day off. "And for last night too," she said. "You're a brave young man."

Carlos blushed.

Before Ms. Otto headed back to her office, I noticed she had a hickey above the collar of her blouse that she had tried to cover up with foundation.

"Have you had lunch yet?" Carlos asked.

"Nuh-uh."

"Let's grab something to eat."

"Okay," I said. "Let me do something first."

I walked up to the table, plucked a balloon from the crystal bowl, and filled it with my breath. The balloon stretched in front of my face, its red skin getting tighter and tighter. When I finished blowing into it, I gave the balloon to Carlos so he could tie it. I uncapped a pen and grabbed one of the cards and started to fill it out.

> Name: *Isabel*
> Age: *17*
> Wish: *He kisses me this time.*

Carlos handed my balloon back to me and I attached the card to it.

"What did you write?" he asked.

"I'm not telling." I walked up to the Plexiglas wall and tossed my balloon in with the others. It bounced on top of another balloon and settled on the hardwood floor.

"That's okay," Carlos said. "I'll find it when I come in tomorrow."

"Don't you dare." I poked his chest playfully.

"I'm just teasing."

"Why don't you do one?" I asked.

"I already did this morning," he said, and looked at the throng of balloons. "It's in there somewhere."

"We should do one together," I suggested.

"Yeah, okay."

Then we were back at the table. Carlos pulled a balloon from the bowl. I grabbed a card and pen.

Name: *Carlos and Isabel*

"Hey," he said. "Who should blow up the balloon, me or you?"

"We both will," I said. "Just blow into it a little and then I'll do the rest."

"Good idea."

"Are you seventeen too?" I asked.

Carlos nodded as he blew into the balloon, his cheeks all puffed out.

Age: *17*

Carlos held the balloon toward me, the navel pinched closed between his fingers. I grabbed it from his hand, careful not to let any of his air seep out, and then blew into it. I thought of my breath and Carlos's breath in the balloon, swirling around each other like two different colors of glitter inside a shaken snow globe. I passed the balloon back to Carlos and he tied the end.

"Okay, now what's our wish?" I held the pen over the card.

"Let me think," he said, facing the entrance of the museum, eyeing the sky.

CARLOS

And I thought, *I wish Snake wakes up soon.*

ISABEL

And I thought, *I wish there's a heaven and Vanessa is there with Gabriel.*

CARLOS

I wish Suji is doing all right, I wish Will doesn't get anyone else pregnant.

ISABEL

I wish Heidi finds someone who's good to her, preferably not Matt Hawkins and his billboard-size forehead.

CARLOS

I wish Mira doesn't think I'm the biggest jerk at Millikan.

ISABEL

I wish I live to be a hundred.

CARLOS

I wish I have a happy life.

ISABEL

I wish Carlos ends up being my boyfriend.

CARLOS

I wish I don't screw things up with Isabel.

ISABEL

"Well?" I asked him. "What's our wish?"

Carlos turned to me and smiled, the balloon between his hands, holding our breath.